My Hidden Secret with a Rodeo Dad

A Second Chance Age-Gap Romance

Nic Spade

Chapter 1

Wrenly

Maybe I shouldn't have run away.

Now that I'm standing in this packed bar, filled with men in cowboy boots and hats, that's all I can think. Each one that walks by me has a wide frame, towers over me by a foot, and looks me up and down as if I'm the most interesting thing they've ever seen.

I don't doubt that I am. All they see every day is a bunch of farm animals, I'm sure — I'm the most action they'll get all night.

Considering I have an interview set up for Monday morning already, I should lift my head up high and deal with my surroundings. There are a few guys laughing around the pool table, and one with blonde hair looks up at me, winks, then pushes his gaze back down to the game. There's nervous energy running through my body — what are the chances that my ex will find me here?

I made it a point to pick the best location to hide in, hoping that he wouldn't find me, but what if I made a mistake? My phone vibrates in my pocket, which only has me huffing in annoyance and ripping it

1

from the back pocket of my skinny jeans. It doesn't surprise me one bit to see a string of text messages a mile long from my ex, waiting to be answered.

Instead of answering them like I'm sure he's hoping, I take a deep breath and push through the crowd while mumbling *excuse me*. A few of the women eye me curiously before curling their lips in disgust, as if I'm not worth breathing the same beer-scented air as they are. I flash them my best smile — my nanny always told me to kill people with kindness, so that's what I live by.

Try to at least.

Most of the time.

I sink into one of the barstools, watching as happy patrons walk up and wave hello to the bartender. There's easy laughter and smiles, as if these people have all known each other for most of their lives, and it has uneasy feelings settling in my chest. I've always felt a little left out of things back home and the only person who ever treated me as something more is the one woman I wish never had to leave me so soon.

God, this is depressing.

There's a live country band stationed on a platform at the front of the room, howling out lyrics about beers and friends, and I roll my eyes before turning back around to wave the bartender down. An older man walks slowly over to me, a frown on his face as he steps in front of me, and I tap my chin.

"You new here?" he asks, crossing his arms over his chest.

I glance around. "Fairly, yes." If fairly means I just got in a few hours ago.

I'm sure this will end up being a major mistake, but I can't back down now. The older man nods slowly, then extends a hand out with a polite smile. "I'm Willie, the owner of this place."

"It's nice to meet you. I'm Wrenly, make me your favorite drink."

He scoffs. "Sweetie, I'm not sure you want me to do that."

I arch a brow and smirk at him. "Now I really need you to." There's a part of me that loves a good challenge, and this is definitely one of those. I'll handle whatever he has for me.

Just as I'm about to take a sip of the drink, my eyes lock on a lone figure sitting at the other end of the bar with his head bowed down to the table. There's no light shining on his face, so he's not playing on his phone, he just really finds the countertop delightful to stare at.

His body stiffens when a woman walks up to him, her hand brushing over his arm with a smile on her face. She says something to him that has his head lifting up, and he shakes it briefly before putting it back down. The woman stalks away with a pout on her face. I chuckle to myself, *so dramatic.*

My body seems to have a mind of its own because before I can talk myself out of it, I'm lifting from my spot at the bar and inching closer to the stranger ahead of me. He still hasn't caught onto my presence yet, not until I sit down in the seat to his left and I watch his frame go rigid. His heavy breathing is making my skin heat up, wondering what it would sound like if he was wishing for release with each one he took.

A release that only I could give him.

This wouldn't be such a bad idea. With the stress of an interview this week, plus everything that happened with my ex, it would be a great time to shack up with a stranger for a night. Somehow, this man sitting alone at the bar is the answer to all my prayers.

He doesn't say anything to me, only keeps his head down and posture stiff under my gaze. I lean back against the countertop, resting my arms over it to gain his attention, but he still doesn't budge. My sigh is loud between the two of us, which has him looking up at me.

I have to suck in a breath of air as his stormy blue eyes look directly into mine, narrowed on me. Narrowed or not, the blue swirling throughout his irises is beautiful. He's wearing what most of the cowboys are in this place — jeans, a t-shirt with a flannel over top, plus the boots and hat — but I still find him to be the most attractive one in here. Judging by the muscles trying to pop out his sleeves, I'd say he's got a great physique, and that has my center *very* aware.

The hard lines of his jaw are so sharp that I could easily lean over and lick the edges of it until he gives in to the pull of whatever the hell this is, but I refrain from doing that. This man has never met me before; I'm a complete stranger and it would be highly inappropriate to jump him like that.

He clears his throat, gaining the attention of my wandering eyes, and there's no hint of amusement in his gaze. No hint of any emotion at all. "Can I help you?" he grinds out, his hand wrapped tightly around the glass of soda he's drinking.

I shake my head with a small smile and shrug. "Not really, just new and thought I'd say hi."

My skin flushes when he gives me a curt nod, then turns his attention back to the top of the table. I nudge him and point to the space he's been staring at since I saw him. "Something fascinating there?"

He growls, stepping up to his feet suddenly and gaining a few head turns from people close by. "I didn't ask for company."

I cross my arms over my chest, face heating at the anger rising through me at the audacity of this man to talk to me like that. "You seemed a little lonely to me, thought you could use a friend." *Or more than friends*, I'd love to say, but that would only make things worse than they already are.

"Well, I'm doing perfectly fine on my own."

My gaze cuts to the middle of the room, where a large group of men and women are line dancing, and I smile at the stranger. "Dance?"

"Pass," he mutters, taking a long swig of his soda. "But, you can go out there on your own, I won't stop you."

I sigh, poking my bottom lip out and fluttering my eyelashes at him in the best way I can. "Please."

He rolls his eyes. "Will you leave me alone if I do?"

"We'll see, depends how good you dance," I say, giving him a wink. There's something about this broody asshole that has me not giving anyone else a second look.

He holds a hand out for me to take, then leads me out onto the floor where eyes bug out at the image before them. Apparently, this is an uncommon occurrence for him.

"Think I could get your name?" I ask.

"Blake," he snaps, letting my hand go as we get in line with all the others and follow the dance movements.

———

Hours have gone by and my body is no doubt glistening with so much sweat I'm sure my clothes are soaked with it, but I can't bring myself to stop. Somehow, I've managed to not only get Blake to dance this entire time, but to also smile once or twice. I've caught his stare on my ass and hips multiple times throughout the dances, and I'm fairly confident about where the night will go for us.

Or at least, I have hope for where it will end. My attention has been solely focused on the way his jeans hug his ass and thighs, and imagining what they would look like without any clothes on them. I'm more than determined to figure that out, especially when he decides in the middle of dancing that he's too hot and takes the flannel off.

My breath hitches at the sight of his tan arms and the muscles trying to rip through the fabric of his shirt, and I sink my teeth into my lower lip. When I glance back up into his eyes, he's staring right at me with a narrowed gaze and walks closer to me.

"You don't want to look at me like that, sweetheart," he rasps out, gaze darting to my lips before coming back up to my eyes.

For a torturous few minutes neither of us makes a move, only darting our gazes to each other's lips, until one of us goes for it. Or maybe both of us. I don't know. All I know is one second I was wishing I knew what his lips felt like on mine, then the next I'm being consumed by him.

Soft, plump, silky, and smooth. That's what his lips feel like, and I can't help but deepen the kiss, even with all these people standing around us no doubt getting in our business. I pull away, panting and smirking at him. "You leaving with me?"

He groans. "I shouldn't." Then he pulls me out of the bar without a backward glance, waiting until we are out on the sidewalk to push me up against the brick wall. "But you've been driving me wild all night, and I don't think I could walk away even if I tried." Before I can respond, he's got his lips back on me and a fire settling deep in my veins.

"Well," he whispers between kisses, "lead the way then." I'm gripping the hem of his t-shirt, more than ready to pull it off him, and nod against his lips.

He pushes off the wall slowly while shutting his eyes and breathing deeply, as if it physically pains him to pull away from me, and I lead him across the street. Luckily, the place I'm staying is two minutes from where we are, or else I'd be stripping him right here in the middle of the sidewalk.

It only takes a couple extra minutes until I unlock my room, and seconds after we walk in for Blake to spin me around and lift me up. My legs instinctively wrap around his waist, hips grinding against him as I devour his mouth, half-convinced my soul is leaving my body in the process.

My hands run down his clothed chest until I reach the hem of his shirt and tug it up. He lifts his arms after pressing my body between him and the wall, helping me get it over his head.

I'm panting, watching as he gives me a devilish grin before leaning down and placing chaste kisses against the curve of my breasts. With no bra on, I have no doubt he can feel my nipples poking through the thin fabric of my shirt.

The only thought I have is that this man has ruined me for anyone else.

Chapter 2

Blake

It's been a long week of interviewing and I have one more to get through today. So far, I'm unimpressed by everyone and it seemed as though they only wanted the job to get closer to me — and that won't fly. Arabella is currently up in her room, where I told her to be for the next hour, so I can get through the first part of the interview alone.

If this interview goes without a hitch, the next part will be meeting my daughter and gauging their interaction. That's not something that's happened so far though, since I haven't trusted any of the other candidates enough to let them meet her — which means it's an automatic no from me, even though I told them I'd call if they got the job. They'll be highly disappointed when I don't give them that call.

The morning sun is shining through the kitchen window, shedding some natural light in one of my favorite places. Rodeoing might be my dream, but there's nothing like cooking homemade meals in a big kitchen like this one. All the appliances are stainless steel and the best of the best, with plenty of open space to move freely in.

Even though the sun is heating my skin, I have no doubt that when I open that door the chilly mountain air will hit me. That's one of the only things that suck living so close to the mountains — the weather is a bitch to get through. Arabella loves it all though, and I'd do anything to see her bright smile every day.

The doorbell rings, so I take a deep breath, fix the suit I'm wearing, and confidently walk toward the door. Suits aren't something I wear often — the fabric is itchy, I'm sweating bullets under it right now, and I'm not even sure what I'm wearing is good enough. I'd be more comfortable in a pair of Wrangler jeans and a Carhartt shirt, but this is my way of looking presentable.

I straighten my spine before opening the door, but any greeting that was going to escape my mouth gets lodged in my throat at the sight of the woman standing before me. She looks much more presentable than she did only a couple nights ago, but the only thing I can imagine is the way my hands fit perfectly over every inch of her body.

She's staring at me with wide brown eyes, her mouth parted in shock, then she mutters a few curses that have me narrowing my eyes. "That's not common language for you, is it?" If so, this interview will be fairly easy. I'm not super strict with the language people use around Arabella, as long as it's minimally used when around her.

My one-night stand from over the weekend shakily extends a hand out to me with a small smile and shakes her head. "Uh, no, sorry. Caught off guard, that's all." She chuckles nervously, her hand still outstretched. "Wrenly Evans, I have an interview for ten."

I nod slowly, trying as discreetly as possible to eye her up. The skirt that hugs her thick thighs, stopping just above her knee, and a blouse that I can't help but recall what she's hiding under it. The red lace bra and panty set she was wearing the other night are still stuck in my head, maybe she's got black on beneath this.

Before she can think I'm some kind of creep, I slip my sweaty palm into hers, and step aside to let her through. I'm not too keen on this situation, but there's a chance she'll be the best option for Arabella this season. The rodeo starts in a few weeks and I've yet to find the right nanny to look after her while I'm on the road, even though I've been interviewing for over a month now.

Wrenly isn't looking at me as though she sees me as eye-candy today though, so I guess that's already a plus for her. All the other candidates focused more on my arms and trying to be flirty with me, rather than what the job actually entailed. There was one woman who was blatantly ogling me, and I made it a point to ask her if she knew what kind of dog food children preferred — just to see if she was paying attention — and she nodded in response.

I lead Wrenly into the spacious living room and watch as she eyes the shelves of pictures with Arabella, her smile brighter with each one she glances at. "Your daughter is beautiful," she whispers before straightening and turning her pink-stained cheeks in my direction. "Sorry, I don't mean to snoop."

Hearing her compliment my daughter is a good start to the interview, it means she's actually interested in being her nanny.

I clear my throat, striding into the room and waving a hand in front of the empty couch. "No problem, you can have a seat." It's hard to keep my gaze down on the list of questions in my lap when she struts over to the spot I'm sitting across from. "There was a resume with your application, but I'd like to know what your experience is with children."

Mostly, I'm asking what qualifies her for this job because I didn't see any previous experience — whether for a daycare or another nanny gig.

She threads her fingers together, setting them gently on her lap as she crosses her legs, and cocks her head to the side. "I'm not sure it counts as experience, but I babysat kids around my neighborhood while growing up."

I blink a few times, then scrub a hand over my face and note the hairs that are starting to pop through my skin. I'll need to shave soon, but not today. "You applied for a nanny position, but have no *real* experience."

Wrenly nods with a sigh, then leans forward with a frown on her face. "I just came to town, and this is the first job I applied to that responded quickly. I need the money, but have no issue with kids."

When she doesn't think I'm convinced after a moment of silence, she says, "I can do hair, I'm very patient, and she'll be in safe hands."

"Are you CPR certified?"

She shakes her head, chewing on her bottom lip nervously. "I'll, uh- I can get certified if that would ease any worries you have."

"Are you able to travel for the position?"

"Absolutely," she says, too quickly for it not to be questionable. I can't ask her about her life though, so I'll keep my mouth shut and continue with the questions.

I nod, then glance at the stairs briefly before turning back to Wrenly with a small smile. "How about I get Arabella down here and we can do a quick trial run?"

"I'm not sure what you mean."

"I'll let you meet Arabella, watch your interaction with her, and that will help me decide what I want to do." I stand quickly, catching her off guard, and frown. "If you get this job, this will be strictly professional."

She scoffs. "Of course, I didn't expect anything different. If I had known you were my interview today, I would've never done anything that night."

Instead of responding, I head toward the spiral staircase across the room and shake my head as soon as I round the corner. Why did it sting when she said she never would've done anything? She's possibly going to be an employee now, it's completely unprofessional.

Arabella's door is slightly open, her light pink walls shining through it, and I gently ease the door open.

She's sitting on the bed Indian style, a colored pencil situated perfectly between her teeth, while she stares at the piece of paper in front of her. Her gaze darts up to me when I tap lightly on her door, a big smile taking over her face. "Hi Daddy," she squeaks out.

"Hey, Bug, come downstairs for a few?"

She nods excitedly, dropping her pencil onto the mattress before jumping out of the bed and fixing her clothes. I bring my hand to the small of her back, guiding her into the living room where Wrenly sits, and wait patiently for some sort of reaction. Arabella is gazing at Wrenly curiously, studying her, before she walks over and plants her hands on her hips.

I watch as the corner of Wrenly's mouth twitches, clearly trying not to smile at the attitude my daughter has copped right now, and it has me bowing my head down with my own smirk. If there's one thing my little girl got from her mother, it's the spitfire attitude of hers.

She's a well-behaved child most of the time, but she has her moments where her mother's personality shines through.

Other than the personality, everything else is all me — her dark curls that span the length of her back that she refuses to let anyone cut, dark-blue eyes, tan skin. She's got my height, something I'm sure will become an issue with the guys when she gets older, but I love it.

"Who are you?" Arabella asks.

I shake my head, then step forward with my gaze narrowed on my daughter. "Bug, we've talked about this. That's not the proper way to greet someone."

My daughter frowns, then rolls her eyes. "Hi, I'm Arabella."

Wrenly can't help but let out a small chuckle of amusement. "Well, hi there, Arabella. My name's Wrenly."

Arabella smiles softly, cocking her head to the side. "Do you know how to do hair?"

"Of course," Wrenly says, her gaze drifting over to me briefly, before going back to my daughter. "I've done my own hair for years."

Arabella nods, her eyes tracking the length of Wrenly's own bright curls. "What about nails?"

Wrenly's hand comes up, showing her the paint that's already chipping off, and smiles. "Actually, I think I'm in need of a new makeover on them. Want to help me?"

I bring a hand to my chin, nodding approvingly at the way she's approaching the subject, and smile when Arabella jumps up and down excitedly. My little girl loves her nail polish collection, and apparently, it's not the same when I let her paint mine. Knowing she's about to have fun with Wrenly is a relief I didn't know I needed.

While I go upstairs to grab her nail polish, Wrenly and Arabella's muffled conversation travels upstairs with me. When I get back downstairs, Arabella rushes up to me and yanks the polishes out of my hand. "Arabella," I say loudly, making her stop in her tracks. "What do you say?"

Manners are a work in progress at the moment, so I make it a point to teach her them as often as I can. She nibbles on her bottom lip while staring at me. "Thank you, Daddy."

I'm long forgotten as she takes a seat next to Wrenly on the couch, placing Wrenly's large hand on her lap. "What color do you want?"

Wrenly smiles brightly at her, almost blinding me with it in the process, and says, "Surprise me, I trust you." Then she leans back and lets Arabella get to work on her nails, not a care in the world that a seven-year-old is currently the one painting them.

I clear my throat, gaining Wrenly's attention, and point my thumb toward the kitchen. "I'm going to look for lunch." If I stand there and watch her interact with Arabella any longer, I might do something drastic.

When I get into the kitchen, I look over my shoulder and catch her dark pools of chocolate locked on mine. She darts her gaze away, but the feeling of them on me still lingers on my skin.

I turn back to look out the window, my gaze focusing on the mountain range ahead, and blow out a rough breath.

Professional. That's all this can be.

Chapter 3

Wrenly

I t's early when I pull up to the large ranch house, one that looks almost identical to the one John Dutton has in Yellowstone, and I blow out a rough breath. I'm surprised I got the job, if I'm being honest. I could tell when we first started the interview that he wasn't sold on me, but I guess after hearing me interact with Arabella he softened to the idea of me being a nanny.

Unfortunately, I was so nervous showing up that I didn't get the chance to look around at the place when I got here yesterday. Today though? I can't deny how gorgeous the ranch looks with the mountain peaks in the distance, standing high in the air, the perfect backdrop for the place.

The flower beds out front compliment the house nicely and look like they are kept up daily. There's a fenced-in area to the right where a few horses are lounging, manes blowing in the wind, and I take a deep breath of the fresh air. Before I can get up onto the porch, the front door swings open and I have to dart my gaze away when a shirtless Blake walks out with a mug of coffee in his hand.

He flinches back, surprised to see me here thirty minutes early, but I figured being early would show him I'm serious about the job. I'm technically not supposed to start for another couple weeks, when the rodeo starts again, but he wanted to get me into the hang of watching Arabella. So, here I am.

"Wrenly, you're early," he rasps out.

It doesn't look like he just woke up, but I can't deny how sleep-filled his voice sounds right now or the way it makes my insides heat up. I nod, pushing a strand of hair behind my hair. "Yeah, I wanted to make a good impression."

God, who says that aloud?

I could've kept that to myself, but that smile he gives me tells me it was a good thing to say, so I let my shoulders slump in relief. He ushers me inside, then rushes upstairs before coming back down with a shirt on. I'm sitting at the island admiring the marble counter-tops when he comes to a stop in front of me. I glance up, locking onto his blue eyes that seem to be much brighter this morning than usual, and I have to look away before I kiss him senseless.

"There's coffee," he says quietly, "if you'd like some."

It feels weird, making myself comfortable in his home, but I get up slowly and head toward the fancy coffeemaker sitting in the corner of the counter. He reaches into the cabinet above me, his chest brushing up against me, and I have to hold my breath until he pulls away and hands me a cup.

"Do you have any creamer?" I ask, surprised that I was able to get the words out so smoothly considering my heart feels like it's about to pop from my chest.

He nods, then heads over to the fridge and produces a small bottle of creamer. While I'm making the coffee, he leans against the counter and watches me with rapt attention. I can feel the sweat dripping down my back from his stare, but I'm not about to open my mouth.

Blake clears his throat. "Have you ever ridden a horse before?"

I shake my head. "No. Not that I haven't wanted to, I just never got the chance."

He nods, then smiles as he pushes away from the counter and walks away. Before he rounds the corner, he turns to look over his shoulder at me. "Guess today is your lucky day then." His graze tracks down my body, assessing what I'm wearing, then he shakes his head. "Do you have anything else to wear?"

I shrug, my nerves threatening to explode. "Maybe, in my car." I'm not counting on it though.

"Just let me know. I'm sure I can find something for you to wear if you don't."

"Yeah," I squeak out, then take a drink of my coffee to cover the nerves up. "I'll go look right after my coffee."

His footsteps fade as he walks out of the kitchen, leaving me to stand alone with my nerves, and I lift a shaky hand to my chest. Maybe I'm being dramatic, but I've never been on a horse and it seems like I'm about to be given a lesson.

The small feet pounding down the steps bring me to attention, and Arabella comes rushing into the kitchen with a bright smile.

I smile brightly at her. "Well, hello beautiful, what are you thinking for breakfast?"

She jumps onto the chair, leaning her elbows on the island with a crazy grin on her face. "Chocolate chip pancakes!"

"Ooh, my kind of girl."

I head into the pantry, noting that there's not a hint of the boxed pancake mix, which means I have to make my own. With my hands full of ingredients, I stumble into the kitchen just as Blake makes his entrance and plants a soft kiss on the top of Arabella's head.

I avert my eyes, setting down the flour, sugar, baking powder, and salt I found.

Have I mentioned that watching him be a dad is sexier than anything I've ever seen?

"You don't have to make food," he says next to me, making me jump in the air. His chuckle echoes through the room. "Sorry, didn't mean to sneak up on you. Here, let me make them."

I shake my head and narrow my eyes at him. "If you do not let me cook in this beautiful kitchen, I will go insane."

Blake throws his hands up in the air with a small smile, then slowly backs up until he's sitting in the seat next to Arabella. They lean into each other, whispering about something I can't hear, other than the small giggles coming out of her mouth. It's strangely comforting, standing at the counter and mixing up breakfast while they're laughing behind me.

Once everything is done, I set their plates down in front of them, then search through the pantry for the syrup and come up empty. I groan, already shaking my head when I get back into the brightly lit kitchen — not that it needs the light, the natural lighting in here is phenomenal. "Please tell me it's not where I think it is," I mutter quickly.

Blake arches a brow. "Where what is?"

"Syrup." Even though I was prepared for it, I scrunch my nose when he points to the fridge. "Seriously?"

He scoffs. "What?"

I roll my eyes as I find the half-empty bottle of syrup, then shut the door with a dramatic sigh. "It's barbaric, that's what!"

Arabella eyes me curiously and cocks her head to the side, then looks up to her dad with bright eyes that match his. "What does barbaric mean?"

Blake chuckles and taps his finger on his chin, trying to think of the best way to describe the word. "Well, Bug, it's basically saying someone is crazy."

She scrunches her nose. "So she's saying it's crazy?"

He nods, trying to hold back a laugh as he takes a sip of his coffee — which I'm fairly certain is cold by now. "Yep, I'm pretty sure that's what she's saying."

Arabella only shrugs, then turns to me. "Oh, okay." She points to the bottle in my hand. "Can I have the syrup now, please?"

I shake my head, then strut over to her with a smile. "Of course, sweetie." Then I send a glare to Blake over her head since he seems to find this entire interaction so funny. "I'll be back in a minute, going to check for proper clothes." I glance down at the outfit I'm wearing, then look back up to him. "What exactly is wrong with this outfit?"

He swallows the bite in his mouth, then points to the shorts I have on. "You should wear pants when riding a horse, along with different shoes. Do you have anything that isn't open-toed?"

I wrack my brain, trying to remember if I grabbed a couple pairs of my boots before running away. "Maybe."

Before he can start asking anymore questions, I hurry out of the house and into the cool morning air where I take a deep breath. He deserves to know that I'm currently on the run, not from anything illegal, just a man who didn't know how to keep his shit together.

There's a triumphant grin on my face when I sift through the clothes sitting on my backseat and I pull out a pair of skinny jeans. But a frown forms when I don't see any boots lying around on the back floor. Maybe I won't be riding a horse after all today. This is probably a sign that I shouldn't be getting on one in the first place.

Blake and Arabella are rinsing their dishes off when I walk through the door, and Blake eyes the jeans in my hand before nodding his approval. I blow out an irritated sigh. "I don't have any other shoes with me."

Blake nods, then leans down to say something to Arabella who quickly runs off and heads upstairs. He nudges his head toward the back door and I follow closely behind him, my eyes widening when I catch sight of the large barn sitting straight ahead. It's white and looks like it's been renovated recently, but I'm more surprised by the room that's stacked to the nines with gear.

He glances at my feet briefly before leaning in and grabbing a pair of cowgirl boots, handing them over to me. "Try those on, let me know how they feel."

I give him a salute, which only has me mentally smacking myself in the face — how embarrassing. The boots fit like a glove, which is odd since he didn't even need to ask what size I wore. When he walks over to me, I study him closely, then look down at the new boots I'm wearing. "How did you know?"

"Know what?"

"What size I wore."

He shrugs, his gaze watching the front door until he sees Arabella run out, then he looks over to me. "I didn't, it was an educated guess."

I hum in response, then smile as his energetic daughter comes barreling down the small hill leading down to the barn. Well, I guess technically stables. She's practically vibrating with excitement and I find myself getting excited as well; this girl could teach me some things.

My heart stalls when Blake leads us over to the fenced-in area where the horses are, his eyebrows rising when he notices my hesitation. "They're not going to hurt you, I promise."

I nod, then take another step closer as he opens the gate for me with a reassuring smile. Is it weird that I can tell which kind of smile he's giving me? *Probably.*

"Okay," he says, leading me over to a lone horse about ten feet away from us. "You're going to hold out the back of your hand, introduce yourself." His hand comes up to the horse's head, petting gently. "This is Storm."

"Just hold my hand out?"

He nods, watching as I do what he says, then smiling when the horse nudges its nose into me. "Good," he whispers, still stroking her. "That means she likes you. Trusts you."

I take in a breath while stroking her the same way Blake just was, moving my body closer to hers with a smile. "Hey there, pretty girl." And that's not a lie. She's got this beautiful silver coat, the black sprinkled in, and a long black mane of hair that stands out. *Stunning.*

"Yeah," Blake chokes out, his eyes darting over to his daughter who looks like a natural on a horse. There's a shift in the air, but I try my best not to pay any attention to it. He looks over to me. "Well, let's try getting on her then, yeah?"

Well, let's hope this doesn't go to shit.

Chapter 4

Blake

Wrenly took to riding Storm fairly easily, but now I'm standing along the edge of the fence while she walks parallel to Arabella on her horse, Brownie. Apparently, as soon as Arabella saw the dark brown color in her horse, it reminded her of one of her favorite chocolate desserts — hence the name. We have four horses — Storm, Brownie, Willow, and Snow.

Arabella giggles loudly from across the field, the sound echoing around me, and I find myself smiling at how well she and Wrenly are getting along. I was worried about Wrenly not having much experience with children, but it seems as though I had her all wrong. There are a few things that need to be done around the house, so I turn the other way and head inside while still making sure to watch them from the windows every few minutes.

Considering Wrenly has no clue how to handle horses, I don't feel comfortable enough just yet not keeping an eye on them out there. I'm sure it will be that way for a little bit, since I'm not entirely used to having someone watch my daughter I don't know. My parents were the ones who used to watch her while I was on the road, but they let me know after my last season that they wouldn't be able to keep watching her.

They want to enjoy life and not have to worry about watching Arabella all the time. Not that they won't take her on some nights, but they don't want to be doing it constantly, and I couldn't argue with them. If there's anything my parents deserve it's time for themselves, and that's exactly what I plan on giving them.

Most people wonder where Arabella's mother is, but that's not a subject I like talking about considering she left the two of us high and dry for someone else. Someone who was better than me, I guess. It's hard to think I was going to give my life to someone who threw me away so easily.

I don't realize I zoned out until the back door shuts beside me and Arabella comes rushing into the back room out of breath. She smiles brightly at me, Wrenly hurrying right behind her with her own smile, before the two girls dash through the house.

I'd ask what the hell they're doing, but I'm not sure I want to know right now. Instead of questioning, I lock the back door and head into the kitchen to get a late lunch made for everyone.

It's surprising, but one of Arabella's favorite things is avocado sandwiches, so I grab an avocado and start slicing it up while a skillet heats on the stove. Giggles echo down the stairs, bringing another smile to my face. I've spent so much time being the only one in Arabella's life, besides my parents and her mother for a short period of time, that I hadn't realized how much I missed her giggles.

Don't get me wrong, I love when I'm the one making her laugh, but it's a whole other thing entirely when someone else makes her laugh. Arabella might have an attitude every now and then, but she's not as outgoing as most people would think. I'm surprised she walked right up to Wrenly yesterday during the interview. I expected to have to nudge her in the direction of her new nanny.

While I heat the avocado sandwiches on the stove, I rummage through the fridge to make sure we have some juice and pull it out. I'm surprised when the girls' footsteps sound through the house, then come to a stop just inside the kitchen as soon as I plate the sandwiches.

"Just in time," I say with a smile as I set the plate of sandwiches on the island.

Arabella immediately lunges for one of the sandwiches, then excitedly hands one over to Wrenly who looks at it with her nose scrunched. I watch in amusement as she sniffs it before taking a small bite, her eyes moving all over the room as she tests the taste of it.

"Good enough for me," Wrenly mumbles before taking a larger bite.

I put a glass of juice for them onto the table and Arabella chugs most of it in one drink. My chuckle echoes through the room. "Thirsty, Bug?"

She nods, then wipes her mouth off and gives me a cheeky grin. "Thank you, Daddy."

Wrenly swallows her bite, then smiles politely at me. "Yeah, thank you, Blake."

"No problem," I say, turning away from her. There's something about her that makes me want to keep looking, but I know that wouldn't be professional, and this is the only way I can think to keep myself from doing so. "Would you like me to take you to the guest house?"

Wrenly pauses. "Guest house?"

I nod. "Of course, you're living on the property during the season."

"Are we not traveling with you?"

"Yes, but not all the rodeos will be far away. Some will be close to here, and you'll end up being here. Knowing you're right across the field would make me feel better."

She hums in response, then stands from her chair and smiles at me. "Well, lead the way I guess."

Arabella follows us through the house and field, skipping alongside us, while humming a song I don't know. Wrenly's silent beside me with her arms crossed over her chest, her eyes cast down at the ground.

We come to a stop outside the guest house door. I grab the key from my pocket and unlock the door, then wave Wrenly inside.

She darts her eyes around each inch of the space, mouth parted as if this is the most beautiful space she's ever seen. When she spins around, I stiffen at the feel of her arms wrapping around me, and the response causes her to immediately push away from me. Her gaze drops to the floor, then she looks over to Arabella who's silently standing beside me with her cheeks flushed.

"This is- it's great," she manages to say. "Thank you."

"It's all yours," I say, handing over the keychain and gesturing to the small space. "Make yourself at home."

Wrenly nods, then sinks her teeth into her bottom lip. My gaze follows the movement, nothing but heat flowing through me, and Arabella's sigh draws my attention back to my surroundings.

I sigh and shake my head. "Alright, Bug, let's give Wrenly some space to get situated, okay?"

Arabella barely glances back at me or Wrenly before she skips back out the door. I run a hand through my hair, watching to make sure Arabella disappears through the front door, before turning my attention back to Wrenly.

She clears her throat. "Sorry for the hug."

I shake my head. "No need. I'll let you get situated, but dinner will be ready around five if you want to join us."

"I wouldn't want to impose," she says quietly. "I can make something quick here."

"That's not necessary if I'm going to be making a meal right across the lawn. You won't be imposing, I promise. I'm sure Arabella would love it if you joined."

Wrenly sighs, looks toward the main house where Arabella ran off to, then nods. "Sure, thank you." She quickly turns around, poking her head through each room without another word directed toward me.

I stand awkwardly in place for a few seconds too long before finally getting the hint and hurrying out of the place.

Arabella is sitting on the couch when I walk through the front door, Bluey shining brightly on the TV mounted above the stone fireplace. There's a small fire going underneath, but it's not too chilly inside that I need to keep up with it.

Arabella turns her attention to me, giving me a smile, before starting her gaze right back to the cartoon.

I walk over to her slowly and sink down onto the couch next to her, then hold my arm out for her to snuggle into. She takes action immediately, not hesitating to rest her head on my chest, and I give her a soft kiss on the head. "How do you like Wrenly, Bug?"

She nods excitedly. "She's so cool, Daddy."

"Well, that's good. I'm glad you're getting along with her." I glance toward the clock, noting there are a few hours until dinner needs to be ready, and clear my throat. "What are you wanting for dinner tonight?"

"Ooh, I think we should let Wrenly try your spaghetti and meatballs!"

I can practically feel the excitement rolling off her, and I let out a small chuckle while tugging her closer into me. There's nothing like holding your daughter on the couch while she watches a cartoon.

"I think that sounds like a plan, Bug, . Would you want to help me make it?"

"Is that a real question?" she asks, looking at me to roll her eyes.

If there's anything I love doing the most with Arabella it's cooking with her. I don't want her to be expected to cook when she finally gets old enough to have her own family, but I want her to be prepared for it. It's one of her favorite things to do with me, aside from riding her horse, and I love the connection it brings between the two of us.

———

There's a soft knock on the door right at five and I hurry to open it, ushering Wrenly inside with a soft smile before rushing back into the kitchen to watch the sauce. Arabella is standing on a step stool in front of the stove, her eyes laser-focused on the pots and pans in front of her, and Wrenly pokes her head between us to get a look at everything.

"Smells amazing in here," she moans, making my body heat from the noise.

"Tell that to the chef next to me," I respond with a smile toward Arabella, who's still putting all her focus on the food in front of us. All that's left is waiting for the sauce to heat up, and my daughter acts like it's a life-or-death mission — I love it. "Would you mind getting the island set up for the three of us, Wrenly?"

Wrenly smiles, her white teeth aligning perfectly, and nods. "Of course." I try my hardest not to glance back and watch as she gets everything situated, but I find my eyes trailing back to her every couple minutes.

"Alright, Bug," I say. "Let's get cleaned up and everything plated, okay?"

She immediately steps down from the stool and rushes down the hall into the half bath to wash her hands. While she gets cleaned up, I walk over to Wrenly's plate and fill it up with the pasta. I grab two wine glasses, then reach into the small wine fridge next to the main one and get the best bottle of red wine I have. "Wine?"

Wrenly nods. "One glass would be great, thank you."

Arabella rushes back through the kitchen and I give her my best stern frown. "You know the rules, Bug."

She sighs and comes to a stop in front of the island. "No running in the kitchen."

I nod. "I let it slide when you went to wash up, but you're going to end up hurting yourself."

"Sorry, Daddy." Then she looks over to Wrenly's plate and pops her bottom lip out. "You already started plating without me?"

I hold out the utensils and smile at her. "Plate mine and yours, baby girl."

While Arabella sets off plating, my neck prickles with awareness and I snap my gaze over to Wrenly to find her staring right at me. Her eyes are glistening and she shakes her head when she catches my stare, then looks back down at her plate.

If only she wasn't the nanny, or I trusted women in general.

Chapter 5

Wrenly

My entire body is vibrating with nerves and I haven't even gotten to the rodeo yet. I'm still sitting inside Blake's house, currently French braiding pigtails into Arabella's hair, while Blake is at the stadium getting prepped for the day. Since the first stop on the rodeo tour is close to his house, he figured we could stay here and leave with everyone else in the morning.

I've been a terrified mess since he told me when the rodeo starts, and all I've done is worry about him getting hurt. I mean, I'm no expert on these things, but I've looked up the average age most bull riders retire and Blake is just hitting the maximum age. What if he can't handle the bulls anymore? At least, not like he used to.

As if reading my mind, Arabella smiles at me through the mirror and says, "Daddy is always the best bull rider. I can't wait to cheer for him."

I smile back at her, lost in her blue eyes that look just like her father's. "I'm sure he is. So you like watching him?"

She nods excitedly, pulling the strands of hair in my grip and making them tug at her scalp. Her yelp is loud, making me flinch in response. "Sorry, you gotta try to stay still, sweetie."

There's a fair amount of silence the next few minutes and she spins around when I'm done, eyeing me curiously. "Are you going to end up with my dad?"

The question is odd, and not one I quite understand. There's no way she could be asking me if I'm going to *date* him. The thought of her thinking that has my cheeks heating up and I quickly turn my gaze away from her.

"Uh, I'm not sure what you mean, Arabella."

She sighs while crossing one leg over the other as if she's a grown adult, and it almost makes me laugh — if it weren't for the serious expression on her face. "Like, are you going to kiss my dad?"

I don't waste any time shaking my head, not bothering to stop until I'm absolutely certain she understands my answer. "I'm only your nanny, sweetie, and I'll be gone once the rodeo season is over."

"Gone?" Her eyes glisten and a tear falls down her face when she blinks slowly. "Why?"

"Well, Arabella, that's what your dad asked me to be here for. I'm supposed to watch you while he's on tour, but there's not much of a reason for me to keep being here when he finishes the season."

Arabella's bottom lip trembles slightly before she bursts into sobs against my chest. I bring my hand to the back of her head, being careful not to mess up her hair in the process, and hum softly into her ear. Even though I may not have the prior work to be standing here, there's nothing I love more than being a shoulder to cry on for children.

I was always misunderstood as a little girl, and I'd hate for Arabella to end up feeling that same way. When her sobs turn to tiny hiccups and she rubs her eyes, I pull away from her slowly with a small smile. "Why don't you tell me what's going on?"

She shakes her head, turning back to the mirror and glancing at herself through it before rushing out, her bedroom door slamming shut behind her. I could let her go, stew in her own depression, but I'm feeling that leaving her alone would be the worse option right now. I'm not sure what's going on with her today, but she's nowhere near the bubbly little girl I've come to love and know since I started spending time with her.

I knock quietly on her door, leaning my head against the hardwood, and frown at the sniffles echoing on the other of it. "I'm okay," she chokes out, her sobs wracking over her body once again, and I opt to barge in rather than wait for permission.

Her glare strikes me though, halting me in my spot, and she turns her back to me with arms crossed over her chest.

The clock shows that we only have a few more minutes before we need to be inside the car Blake's sending for us, and I huff out an irritated sigh before inching closer to her. I bend to eye level on the floor, pushing my head beneath where her own is bowed down, and she merely blinks at me.

"Arabella, what's going on?" I ask, getting worried now. I'd hate to have to make a call to Blake and let him know Arabella isn't doing too well right now, especially when he's been talking about the season starting nonstop.

She stares at me and shrugs. "Why can't my daddy be good enough for anyone?"

The question has my heart crashing to the ground on the spot, and I don't care if anyone sees just how broken I am by her question. It's a good one, especially since I've gotten the pleasure to know Blake as not only a stranger, but as a boss, and I have nothing but good things to say about him. So, why is there not a woman standing by his side tonight like there should be?

This isn't my life to worry about. Instead of giving her the answer I'd like, I bring my hand to her cheek. "I think he's good enough for you, isn't that right?"

"I guess so," she mumbles, still not in the greatest mood.

I hold my hand out to her with a smile. "What do you say we get to this thing and give him our best cheers from the stands? Think we can be the loudest ones there?"

It's crazy how quickly children can wipe away their tears, as if the ones they just got done spilling mean nothing to them. Arabella wipes at her eyes and gives me that bright smile I was worried wouldn't appear again today, then nods at me. "Totally!"

———

If I thought I was in heaven seeing Blake every day, I'm not sure I knew what heaven was at the time. Still not sure, but that's not the point. Each person in attendance has a nice cowboy hat, jeans, and their asses look fantastic. But it's not them that steals all my attention, not at all.

Standing just outside the fence, leaning over as he talks animatedly with an older man, Blake is showcasing all of his goods tonight. There's something extremely sexy about the way he's sporting the dark outfit — dark jeans, black top, black vest, and black everything else. Who knew someone could look so good in black?

Arabella tugs gently on my hand, pointing towards her father with a bright smile, and I hurry us through the growing crowd until we get next to him. The older man smiles politely at me, before kneeling on the ground and tipping his cowboy hat at Arabella. "And who is this young lady?"

Blake shakes his head with a chuckle. "Bud, this is my daughter, Arabella, you met her a few years ago."

Bud's eyes grow wide. "Why, you've grown a lot since the last time I saw you, sweetie." He glances over at me, eyes studying me in a way that has me fidgeting uncomfortably. "And you are?"

I hold a hand out to him with a smile. "Wrenly, the nanny."

He nods in understanding, then slips his hand into mine and gives me a firm handshake. His gaze darts between Blake and me, a gleam in his eyes that I can't decipher, and Blake says his goodbyes before leading us over to the gate where he's going to be.

"Get here okay?" he asks, pulling Arabella into him while staring at me.

"Yep," I squeak out when another cowboy walks past us, his eyes burning a hole into my chest. This is what I get for trying to look like every other woman in attendance — I'm sporting a push-up bra that has the top of my breasts poking out of the tank I'm wearing with a pair of skinny jeans and light brown cowgirl boots. The only thing I need now is a cowgirl hat, but I'm still attracting much more attention than I thought I would without it.

Blake glares at the guy's back, eyes turning black as coal, and it has a shiver rolling down my spine.

I shake my head slightly. *He's not jealous, you idiot.* I'm not sure why I would think he is in the first place; he was pretty clear what kind of relationship we would have during this time.

He clears his throat, seeming to come down from whatever had made him angry for a second, and says, "I already saved tickets for you two. All you have to do is head to the ticket office and give them my name."

I nod. "Thank you."

Arabella's curious eyes dart around the stadium, studying each and every man that walks past, when Blake kneels in front of her. His hand comes up to the braid and he pinches the strands of hair at the bottom with his fingers. "Who did your hair?"

"Wrenly. She does it so good, doesn't she, Daddy?"

Blake chuckles and nods, placing a small kiss to the top of her head before standing up. "She does, Bug." He stuffs his hands into the front pockets of his pants, eyes searching through the crowd as if looking for someone specific. I follow his gaze when it narrows, noting the guy who walked passed us only moments ago, and cock my head to the side.

There seems to be some bad blood there, but that's not my business. Instead of asking Blake questions that I don't deserve an answer to, I reach my hand out for Arabella and nudge my head toward the ticket area. "How about we head to our seats?" Judging by the line outside of the booth, I'm willing to bet it will be time for the rodeo to start as soon as we get to our seats.

Arabella nods and eagerly wraps her hand around mine, then gives her dad a big smile that would light up anyone's day.

Blake pulls out his wallet, shoving a few twenty-dollar bills in my hand, and I look up at him with my eyebrows raised in question. He nods toward the money. "For food, or anything else you guys want. Should that be enough?"

I chuckle. "More than enough, thank you." Before I can stare into this man's eyes for any longer, I hurry through the rowdy country folk and get into the back of the ticket line.

When I get closer to the front, a large body towers over Arabella and me, his shadow casting a nice shade over us. I turn toward the person, my eyebrows jumping when I see it's the guy who was checking me out. He smiles at me, then walks away toward his own section of the stadium, but before he vanishes his gaze snags on me again and he winks at me.

Winks at me.

My heart stutters in my chest, but I try not to let the reaction show-case itself. The man might be attractive, but he doesn't have anything on Blake and his wide frame, or bright eyes. It seems as though the only thing I can ever pay attention to is the deep shade of his eyes. That's my luck since I have to look at them every day.

The closer we get to the ticket booth, the easier it is to breathe, as if being close to Blake in any capacity makes me lose that function entirely.

Am I screwed? Probably.

Do I care? Sure. Maybe.

Chapter 6

Blake

Wrenly was so happy tonight, but the flames that flowed through me from seeing it were doused with water as soon as my gaze found Erica standing along the fence. It angered me, to watch her smile across the stadium at Dennis, my competitor, because it shows how much I wasn't enough for her. That someone, somewhere, will always be searching for more.

That anger is how I find myself pushing open Arabella's door, staring at her small form curled into a ball while she sleeps peacefully in bed. I smile softly, then shut the door until only a small crack is left in it and leave the hallway light on in case she wakes up while I'm in the barn.

I slip my jacket on, then step outside and take a deep breath of the crisp air, my gaze tracking over to the guest house across the lawn. There's a small light on in the living room and I can see the silhouette of Wrenly through the white curtains. The image of Arabella on her shoulders flows through my head, releasing some of my tension, but it's immediately replaced by one of Erica smiling at Dennis.

And the anger comes right back.

It wasn't long after I lost against Dennis that she came up to me, asking me for a divorce without telling me why. When I caught her kissing Dennis late one night — she thought I was asleep — I understood exactly why she wanted the divorce. I went years winning the rodeos, and as soon as I lost, she went straight to him. This is my year to win again, for Arabella and myself.

The blood in my veins is boiling over before I even get through the sliding doors of the barn, my gaze immediately focusing on the large punching bag hanging from the ceiling. This is my way of letting out all my stress, and I made sure to put it far enough away that it wouldn't wake Arabella up late at night. I grab the gloves on the bench, always lying there at the ready for when I come in, and slip my hands through them.

My fist snaps out, connecting to the bag with a loud bang, and a millimeter of my anger dissipates. Just the echo of the bag makes me feel better, but it's still not enough for me to stop. Before I sweat too much, I slip my jacket off and throw it onto the barn floor along with my t-shirt. There's nothing worse than a shirt sticking to you, plus the cool air feels glorious and helps me cool off without having to take a break.

It takes about thirty minutes before I'm out of breath, my chest pumping up and down with each rapid breath I take, and most of my anger has gone away. I walk over to the bench and lean my head back against the wall behind me, closing my eyes while I get my breathing under control.

Something clatters loudly onto the floor, causing me to jump up immediately and my eyes land on Wrenly standing about twenty feet away with her eyes glued to my glistening chest.

There's a rake lying on the ground at her feet, but it doesn't seem to be phasing her one bit as her eyes slide down the rest of my body. Her tongue darts out over her bottom lip before she sinks her teeth into it. She doesn't even register my steps inching closer to her, and even though I'm trying to will my body to stop moving, I just seem to keep cutting into the distance between us.

When I finally reach her and bring my hand to her chin, her eyes finally meet mine and she shakes her head from my grip. I'm not having any of that right now though, not after the way she looked at me just now. My head is screaming at me to turn around and go back to the bench, but every other part of me is telling me to ignore the screams.

And that's exactly what I do.

I put my fingers back under her chin, lifting her face up to mine, and she parts her lips while darting her gaze to mine. Before I can talk myself out of it, I lower my face down to hers until my lips brush against hers. She opens for me immediately, her lips feeling just as soft, if not softer, than they were the first night we spent together. I wrap my arm around her waist, pulling her into me, and all the blood rushes to my dick.

Her soft moan only has me coming more undone as I deepen the kiss, pushing my tongue between her lips and soaking in the warmth. She brings her hands up to my chest, grazing her finger over my abs, and my breath hitches. I take a step back, stepping right onto the handle of the rake, and everything comes into focus.

"Shit," I mutter before pulling away from her, leaving a couple feet of distance between us. "Uh, I-" She's staring at me with narrowed eyes, and I run a hand through my hair and glance back at the house. "I have to get back inside, Arabella's in there alone."

She doesn't even get a word out before I rush past her. I grab my shirt and jacket, then I rush up the lawn and throw the front door open.

As soon as I shut the door softly behind me, I walk over to the window facing the barn and watch Wrenly stand there for a few more minutes before walking back up towards the guest house.

This isn't right.

She works for me, it was beyond unprofessional for me to kiss her like that. But damn if I don't want to do it all over again. I'm not sure if it was lip gloss or chapstick, but whatever it was, it tasted like peaches. And now I can't think of anything better than buying peaches from the store, even though I hate them. I push away from the window slowly, then hurry up to my room for a quick shower.

Except, the only image in my head as the hot water cascades down my body is what I would do to Wrenly if she were in here with me. I rush through my routine, then step out of the shower and wrap a towel around my waist. For the first time in a while, I try to conjure up an image of Erica smiling at someone who isn't me, but it does nothing to help my aching dick.

I blow out a rough breath, then aggressively pull the mirror open and grab my toothbrush. When I get back into the room, instead of going straight to the bed like I should, I walk over to my window and peer down at the guest house.

She's still awake, if the bright light shining is any indication. I catch sight of her and watch as she sits up in the bed. Her head falls back against the headboard, her mouth parted, and I'm breathing heavily at the idea of what she's doing under the blanket that's covering her. I watch as she lifts her legs up slightly, giving herself a better angle, and I'm starting to wonder why I thought transparent curtains were a good idea for those windows.

I growl, the sound so foreign coming up from my throat that it has me jumping in the air slightly, but not enough to get out of the window. Not enough to keep my eyes from watching Wrenly as she plays with herself. It would be respectful if I moved away, but is it a coincidence that after I kissed her she's pleasuring herself?

Is she thinking about me as she uses her fingers? Or does she have a favorite toy that she brought here with her, and she's using that instead? Maybe she's picturing me using it on her instead of herself, my fingers pushing into her and helping her get there faster.

I bring my hand to the front of the towel, gripping the length trying to poke out of the fabric, and I groan at the contact. Would Wrenly squeeze me tightly while I wrapped her hair around my hand, her mouth popping open to pleasure me? The thought has me squeezing my eyes shut, an image already flowing through my mind and my hand pumping up and down my hard length.

I'm not even sure when I dropped the towel to the floor, but that's not what I care about right now. By the time my release comes and I open my eyes, the window below is dark and I'm left cursing at myself for giving in to the thoughts. This isn't what Arabella needs. I mean, what would she think if she knew I was thinking about her nanny in a totally wrong way?

I grab the towel, wiping my release from my hand before throwing on a pair of shorts and getting comfortable under the blankets on my bed. I'm sure things will be weird in the morning, but here's to hoping it won't be.

Soft footsteps in the hall alert me to Arabella, then she pushes open her door while wiping the sleep from her eyes. I open my arms and smile at her. "Get in here, Bug."

She does, coming up onto the bed and laying her head on my chest. "What woke you up?" I ask.

She shrugs, snuggling closer to me and closing her eyes slowly. It only takes minutes for her breathing to even out and I smile softly while running my fingers through her soft curls. Most of the time her hair is tough to handle, but not after she gets a bath. I sink into the pillows, resting my chin against the top of Arabella's head, and try to push the thoughts of Wrenly away.

For the first time since Erica left me, I fall asleep picturing a pair of chocolate eyes looking back at me. And it's more peaceful than I would've hoped, than I would've thought it could be.

———

"*Daddy,*" Arabella whispers in my ear, waking me up in the best way possible. I try to keep my face neutral, not wanting her to realize I'm awake, and it takes everything in me not to chuckle when she sighs against me. "Wakey, wakey."

Before she can manage to get a reaction out of me, I pop up and she jumps back. The glare she sends me only has me cracking up, then reaching out to pull her on top of me.

"Daddy," she says, kicking her little feet at me while missing completely. "Let me go!"

"I thought you wanted me to wake up?" I ask, bringing my fingers under her rib cage and tickling her.

Her giggles bring a bright smile to my face, making me realize there's no place I'd rather be than in this big bed with her laughing in my arms. My mornings are the best because of her, and it only makes me sad that Erica couldn't bother to be part of that.

I ease up on the tickles and hug my girl closer to my chest, breathing in her scent, then lift up from the bed with her still in my arms. "Time for some breakfast before we head out."

I almost come to a halt when I see Wrenly standing in the kitchen, a breakfast spread already sitting out on the counter, while she sips a cup of coffee. I'm pretty sure this woman is going to be the death of me.

Chapter 7

Wrenly

I 'm nervously rummaging through what little clothes I brought with me, my mind running back to the kiss Blake and I shared last night. I thought he was into it, there's no doubt I was, but he acted as if it meant nothing.

That's not what it felt like though. The way his lips molded perfectly with mine, his arm wrapping around me and pulling me closer, and the tent in his pants that brushed against my stomach.

I shake my head, putting the last of my clothes into a duffel bag, then throw it over my shoulder. My alarm went off early, mostly because I wanted to show Blake it wouldn't be weird for us today, so I'm going to get breakfast ready before he and Arabella wake up.

When I first started, Blake showed me where he keeps the spare key outside the house, so I reach under the potted plant next to the door and unlock it before putting the key back. It's quiet when I step inside, letting me know I woke up earlier than Blake and Arabella, and I rush into the kitchen. Since Arabella loves pancakes, I opt to make chocolate chip ones just like I did my first day on the job.

It's just as I'm plating the pancakes that Blake and Arabella walk into the kitchen, the beautiful little girl snuggled close to her dad's chest. Blake's bare chest, which I'm noticing a lot more than I probably should be. I manage to dart my eyes away, instead focusing on the coffee I made for myself moments ago.

Blake clears his throat, gaining my attention. "You didn't have to make breakfast."

"Chocolate chips!" Arabella says excitedly from the chair, reaching over to dump syrup onto her pancakes.

I chuckle, then give Blake a small smile and shrug my shoulders. "It wasn't too much."

He takes a deep breath, his eyes falling on Arabella before coming back to me. "Uh, about last night."

"We don't have to worry about that right now. It was a mistake, right?"

"Uh, yeah." He coughs, then nods. "For sure."

Before the conversation can go any further, Blake strides over to the island and gets his plate situated for himself. His movements are stiff, like something's bothering him, and I'm itching to figure out what's going on.

It can't be our conversation, right?

I mentally curse at myself, then walk over and grab the plate with my own pancakes on it. Since I made the comment about syrup being in the fridge, Blake made it a point to leave one in it for him and Arabella while leaving another in the pantry for me. There's a weird rush of warmth flowing through me at the idea of him thinking about me and what I told him, but I'm sure it's only to make his employee comfortable.

Once we are finished with our food, Blake takes Arabella over to the couch and places her between his legs. I lean against the kitchen counter, watching as he pulls apart strands of her hair in the exact same way I would if I were French braiding it. He starts off slow but eventually goes at a quicker pace while asking Arabella to stop moving.

I never thought it would be so hot watching a man do a little girl's hair, even if that little girl is his daughter. My panties are going to flood the longer I stand here and stare, which would be terrible for everyone involved.

Instead of watching them any longer, I grab the duffel I dropped by the front door and walk outside to put the bag in the car we'll be taking on the trip.

When I get back inside, Blake is already standing in the living room with his and Arabella's bags at his feet, smiling down at her as if she's the brightest thing in the world. I can't even deny that thought — she really is the brightest person.

Blake glances up at me and gives me a short nod, letting me know it's time to head out. I wonder what being on this trip will be like. Will it help the attraction I feel towards him?

"We all ready?" he asks.

I nod, feeling awkward standing by the door. He pulls the straps of the bags over his shoulder, then nudges Arabella out the door without looking at me once. Maybe the breakfast thing didn't do what I thought it would. I wanted this trip to be smooth sailing, no amount of awkwardness, but it looks like that might not happen.

He holds the door open, then waves a hand out in front of him to let me go out ahead of him while he locks the house up. I run through a mental checklist in my head, making sure I got everything I need, before hurrying toward the car where Arabella is already sitting inside.

Blake pulls open the back door of the car, double-checking that Arabella is buckled in properly, then walks to the driver's side door and sinks into the plush seat. It takes everything in me not to turn my head and watch as he situates himself in the seat, but somehow I manage to keep my gaze turned out the window.

———

Two hours into the drive, my phone pings with a new text and I lift it from where it lays on my thigh. My eyebrows jump up when I see it's a text from my ex, begging me to come back, and I roll my eyes before putting the phone back down. If there's one thing I refuse to fall for it's the act Sean puts on, no matter how we were together I won't budge on where I stand.

"Everything okay?" Blake asks quietly, since Arabella fell asleep about thirty minutes ago.

I scoff. "Sure."

"Want to talk about it?"

"I'd rather not," I mumble before going back to staring out the passenger window, just like I have been for most of the drive. It's taken everything in me not to watch Blake as he cruises along the interstate, to stare at his jaw clenching when he curses at someone driving like an idiot. He already made me ache for him when I watched him braid Arabella's hair with ease, I'd rather not go through that again just by watching him drive.

The silence is uncomfortable, and it only has me sighing and glancing over at the side of his face. "It's my ex," I say, watching for some sort of reaction but getting none. "He's begging for me to come back to him."

Blake hums in response, but says nothing otherwise.

"I ran away." It's not something I wanted to admit, but I guess it's something my employer should've known. "Because of him."

He lets out a pensive chuckle, a deep vibration that flows right through my core, and I have to clench my thighs together. "Sounds... rough."

"Sure is."

"I have an ex too that makes me angry," he blurts out, something I'm sure he didn't want to say, but it seems as though this car ride is bringing out all the things we've been holding inside.

"Yeah? Wanna talk about it?"

He shakes his head, not taking his gaze off the road in front of us. "Not particularly." I nod, assuming it's the end of the conversation, but he lets out a rough sigh. "She's more than an ex. More like ex-wife."

"What happened?"

Blake shrugs, flipping his turn signal to move around someone, before going back to the right side of the road. "Wasn't good enough for her I guess."

"Seems like we are in the same position."

I shouldn't enjoy having this conversation with him, not when it's about both of our exes who seem to think other people are better than the two of us, but I can't help the comfortability rolling through me. There are still a few more hours left of the drive before we reach the hotel where everyone on the rodeo circuit is going to be held up, but hopefully it can keep going like this.

"There's a guy, he beat me one year and she practically begged for a divorce after," he says and I watch as his hands tighten around the steering wheel from the memory.

"Blake, you don't have to talk about this." I can't imagine how hard it must be.

"No, I should, it might help me get over it." I highly doubt that, but I'll let him do what he thinks is good for him. "She asked for a divorce, or more like demanded it, and I was confused as to why." He chuckles, as if the memory is funny, but I'm willing to bet it's anything but. "Then I caught her outside our home, kissing Dennis, the guy who won against me, and I understood why she wanted one."

I'm not even sure what to say about this. He's acting all calm and collected about it, but judging by the way his face is getting red, I'm having a hard time believing it's nothing to him. There's also a small part of me that wants to beat the shit out of this woman for hurting such an amazing man and his daughter. Which brings the reason for my next question. "Is Arabella her daughter?"

Blake scoffs. "Barely." Then he sighs and nods curtly. "But, yes."

In the weeks that I've been here, I've yet to see another woman besides Blake's mother and myself walk through his front door. What kind of woman, and mother, could leave such a sweet little girl without a care in the world?

I turn my head, glancing back at Arabella's peaceful face as she leans her head against the window. No wonder she accepts me so easily, she's probably missing the love of a mother in her life. The thought only makes me want to give her more attention than I have been — if that's even possible.

"I'm sorry," I whisper while reaching my hand over the glove compartment and giving his arm a gentle squeeze. "Is she okay?"

He shrugs. "As far as I can tell. I try my best to be both parents for her, and I'm going to continue doing that for her." The car goes silent for a few minutes while I ponder what he said, then he breaks the silence by asking, "What about your ex?"

"Uh, I'm not sure that's a story for right now." I hate that he's choosing to open up to me while there are some things I'm not comfortable talking about. "Sorry, I don't mean to be rude after you just spilled everything to me."

"Nah, don't worry about it. I understand more than you think."

It only takes another hour before Arabella wakes from her nap, asking if we can stop somewhere for a restroom break and food. Blake takes us to a McDonald's, silently eating a burger while I share a twenty-piece with Arabella. I'm worried he's upset that I didn't open up to him, and hope I can bring it up to him when we get to the hotel.

Before we head back on the road, Blake stops at a gas station to fill the car up, then heads back onto the interstate. There's country music flowing softly through the car and I smile at Arabella humming along behind me, then reach over and turn the volume up on it. When I glance up at Blake, the corner of his mouth is tipped up into a small smile and he relaxes into the seat.

I have a feeling traveling isn't going to be so easy when I have to sit so close to him, not when I can feel his body heat from over here. It only makes me want to inch closer to him and lay my head on his arm, but I fight the urge and instead angle my head closer to the sound of Arabella's humming with my own smile.

This is something I could get used to... and that's a very bad thing.

Chapter 8

Blake

Every muscle in my body is tight right now, but that still wouldn't stop me from carrying Arabella while she's asleep. Wrenly is walking ahead of me, ready to unlock the door to let me through, and she gives Arabella a soft smile as I walk past.

Today was one of the best days in a while. I got nearly one hundred points, and I can't help but think it's all because of the woman who was standing in the crowd with my daughter.

It seems as though they've already formed a routine, even though it's only the second night, and that had me feeling a certain way all night. I'm sure it also helped that Erica wasn't in the crowd, considering she never traveled with me either. I'd be surprised if she wasn't with other men behind Dennis's back while he's on the road.

That's not what I want to be worrying about right now though, not when Wrenly walks over to me and holds her arms out. I cock my head to the side. "What?"

She chuckles, extending her arms out further. "Let me put her to bed, you're hurting and you've been through a lot tonight. I'll get her situated while you take care of yourself."

I steal a glance at Arabella and give her a soft kiss on the forehead before placing her in Wrenly's arms. "Thank you," I whisper before heading in the direction of the bathroom, while she heads into one of the two rooms to put Arabella into bed. There weren't many other rooms open, since all of the cowboys entered into the rodeo reserved a room along with anyone in the audience that needed one.

With that being said, there are only two rooms, and that means I'm sleeping in bed with Arabella while Wrenly gets a room to herself. Not that I mind, but I'm not sure I'll be able to stop wondering what she's doing alone. My mind goes back to when she first walked into the stadium with Arabella, and the way the jeans she wore for the night were hugging her delicious curves.

All I could think was that I wanted to run my tongue over those curves, but I'm trying my hardest to tame the temptation. It's not going as well as I'd like it to. Right about now my feet are itching to rush into her room and peel the clothes off her body, find out what she's wearing underneath, but I'm fighting myself not to move.

An ice bath would feel great right now, especially for all the strain my muscles have gone through tonight. Since I don't have ice handy, I turn the temperature on the water completely cold and fill the bathtub up.

It hurts to remove my clothes, but once I do, I start by dipping my feet into the water and slowly sink down. I suck in a breath, the sudden chill from the water seeping into my bones, then blow out a relieved breath once my muscles get used to the cold.

The contrast of hard-worked muscles and then the relaxtion that ensues after is one of the best parts about doing the rodeo, aside from being on the bull itself, and I just lean my head back with my eyes closed. The floor creaks under Wrenly's footsteps and I keep my ears peeled for any odd noises, but all that I hear is the TV. I'm not sure why I thought she'd do something crazy while being in this hotel room with me.

After spending about ten to fifteen minutes soaking in the water, I finally lift myself out and grab a towel to dry off. I curse at myself when I realize I never grabbed a new change of clothes for myself, and pull the door open slightly to see what Wrenly's doing. Her gaze is pointed right at the TV, so I quickly exit the bathroom and hurry into the room I'm sharing with Arabella.

As soon as I slip a pair of pajamas on, I give Arabella another kiss on the forehead and head out into the sitting room with Wrenly. She doesn't turn her head toward me when I walk in, which means she must be watching something exciting. My suspicions are confirmed when she jumps as I flop onto the couch next to her.

"Jesus," she mutters with a glare aimed at me. "Think you could be a little more careful?"

I shake my head with a smile. "Not my fault your eyes are glued to that thing."

"She still asleep?"

There's something about the way she asks about Arabella, even though she doesn't have to. As if she cares about my daughter, outside of being her nanny, and that's a terrible predicament for me.

I run a hand through my wet hair and nod with a small smile. "Still out like a light." I'm not counting on her waking up anytime soon, especially with everything we've had to do since arriving at the hotel.

Wrenly tucks her legs under her, causing her ass to stick out a little more and it takes everything in me not to groan at the sight. I'm not sure what it is about her that has me looking at her this way. Usually, I'm the one-and-done kind of guy after what happened with Erica, but this woman has pushed straight into my life and I'm not sure what I feel anymore.

I want to be able to be with another woman, but I'm worried my past will come to bite me in the ass or the woman won't want to deal with a child and it keeps me from making that leap. But with Wrenly, it seems as though everything comes naturally. She makes me smile with the attention she gives Arabella, sets my body on fire when she's near, and causes me to open up about something I haven't talked about in a long time.

In the beginning, when everything first happened, I went a little insane and had to go see a therapist. It's not something I broadcast because men are supposed to be seen as strong, and people knowing I've had to get help mentally isn't something they'd necessarily agree with — according to my agent at least. But, I had to get help, and that's the last time I ever talked to anyone about what Erica did to me.

Although it didn't help in the way I wanted it to, it still felt nice for someone else to know what happened between me and Arabella's mother. My mother doesn't even know the situation. She has her assumptions and always tries to get me to admit if they're right or not, but I never budge. I'm not willing to accept I'm not good enough, and admitting that I wasn't out loud is something that hurts me — so I try not to do that and keep it bottled up instead.

My anger is the only release I ever really have, along with my punching bag. Here lately, bull riding has also been my stress release, and I'm worried it's going to make a fool out of me. I blink when Wrenly waves her hand in front of my face, her eyebrows scrunched in concern.

"You okay?"

I sigh and nod. "Yeah, what were you saying?"

"I asked how you got into bull riding."

Perfect, just the type of thing I needed to get my mind off my sucky life. I smile at her, thinking back to all the memories. "My uncle."

She chuckles and it has my body reacting to the sound of it, so I resituate myself on the couch and place a pillow over my lap to hide evidence of it. "I could go with a little more than that."

"He was my dad's brother, taught me everything I know about horses and bull riding. It was like an instant connection and I knew it's what I wanted to do with my life before I even got out of high school."

She smiles, but it quickly falls. "Was?"

This is one of the toughest things to talk about, especially since I was there the night he died and had to witness it. "Yeah, he uh, he died about ten years ago during a rodeo." I shake my head, eyes already stinging with tears, but I push them away. "I was his number one fan, made my parents take me to all the rodeos and they never let me down. It was a thrill to sit in the stands, watching him do his thing on the bull, but something went wrong during the last one and the bull ended up trampling him."

When I glance up at her, there's a single tear rolling down her cheek that I instinctively reach out and swipe away. She shakes her head, prompting me to flinch away from her, and says, "That's awful, I'm so sorry you had to see that, but I'm also happy you found your passion." She brushes a strand of hair behind her ear and clears her throat. "Do you ever worry that the same thing will happen to you?"

That's not something that a lot of people ask me. Sure, they think it most of the time, but everyone assumes that I'll get defensive if they ask. Instead of berating her for asking me such a thing, I nod and blow out a rough breath. "Every single time I'm out there, but I also know I'm one of the best at what I do and trust that I'll get through unscathed."

Maybe not completely unscathed, but at least not sent to the hospital in critical condition or anything. My motivation every time I get out there now is a little girl who calls me dad, and that's the only motivation I need.

Unless it's not. I will the thought to go away and glance over at the digital clock sitting on the dresser along the wall. "I should get to bed." I'm suddenly feeling too comfortable talking about this with Wrenly, and I'm not sure I like it right now. I've never been enough romantically for anyone in my life. I'm not sure that will change with her and I'm not going to let myself believe that's the case.

She nods, then relaxes into the couch and focuses on the TV, her eyes not glancing over at me once as I walk away. I should apologize for my abrupt departure, but part of me can't right now after everything I just told her. Sure, I've gotten asked the question during interviews, but I never answered them in the way they hoped. I give them the generic one about my uncle being a bull rider and he taught me everything I know, but I've never mentioned anything about his death.

What the hell is it about this woman that has me opening up about everything bad in my life, as if I've known her all of it? I scrub a hand over my face, tiredness finally taking over as I sink into the mattress beside Arabella who's still passed out, and stare up at the ceiling for a minute. With nothing else happening, the TV still echoes through the hall and I groan at the thought of Wrenly sitting out there alone.

God, why do I care so much about this?

All I need to do is beat Dennis this year, then I'm done. Wrenly just had to go and make me remember why I started this dream in the first place, but is it enough to have me going back next year, or should I still retire once I win?

There's no doubt in my mind I'm winning this time and I'll shove it right in Dennis and Erica's faces with a smile, while celebrating with my favorite little girl... *girls* sounds nicer though, and I fall fast asleep with a smile on my face at the thought.

Chapter 9

Wrenly

It's been a weird week. Blake and I had a great conversation last week when I asked him about bull riding and how he got into it, but I've been missing him in the mornings since. There's a small break in between events, so he doesn't necessarily need me right now, but I have nowhere else to go. Which sucks because I find myself searching for him every day and get upset when I come up empty.

Arabella has been in the kitchen waiting for me a couple times this week in the mornings, before her dad wakes up, but that's the most I've seen her too. Blake has a pool; maybe I can go for a dip in it and get out of my head. But what if Blake's out there with Arabella? Last I remember he was going to town with her, but I'm not sure if they've gotten back yet.

I shake my head, then grab my phone with a loud groan. Seeing Sean's name on the screen immediately makes me sick, especially since he thinks it's so easy to just run back to him. As if he didn't hurt me enough to make me run away. What is it about men that makes them think they can do whatever the hell they want to us, but the moment it happens to them they're livid about it?

God, this is the last thing I need right now.

You know in the cartoons when they have a light bulb moment and think of something genius? That's about how I feel right now when I think about the night I walked in on Blake in the barn, beating at the punching bag hanging from the ceiling. It seemed to do a lot for him, considering he kissed me that night, so maybe it will do the same for me.

It doesn't hurt to find out.

I'm sure I packed a pair of workout clothes somewhere in here, I just have to rummage through everything and find them. Usually, I pride myself on being a pretty tidy person, but ever since I came here my clothes have been thrown throughout the small bedroom and bath-room floor. Maybe a little cleaning could help me out too.

I pull aside different clothes, until I come across my black sports bra at the bottom, then walk over to one corner of the room and try to locate a pair of yoga shorts. It shouldn't be too hard to find. I like being comfortable at night and I know I packed a decent chunk of clothes appropriate to workout in.

As soon as I find the shorts, I change into the clothes and twist my hair into a high ponytail, then grab the tennis shoes sitting next to the front door. The cool air that hits me when I open the door has me wrapping my arms around myself as I head in the direction of the barn.

Shit.

What if he's in here though?

I shake my head, then lift it up high and round the corner. It's empty, which has my shoulder relaxing and I let out a relieved sigh. The bag is hanging there, calling to me, so I set my phone down on the bench Blake sat on that night and walk over to it. The first swing has me wincing slightly at the impact, but I swing at it again and the anger I was feeling dissipates a bit at a time.

It doesn't take long before I'm struggling to breathe, baby hairs sticking to my head from sweating so much, and Blake clears his throat from the doorway. I jump and bring my eyes slowly up to him. "Sorry, I know this is yours, just really needed it right now."

He nods, then walks further into the empty space and nudges toward the gloves lying on the bench. "No problem, I suggest using the gloves next time though." Then he sighs and rubs a hand over his face. "I was actually looking for you."

I arch a brow. "Really? I thought you'd been avoiding me." I've never been known as one to hold my tongue. If I have a thought, I don't hold it in.

Blake chuckles. "Yeah, I'm sure it seemed that way. No, I've been going to my mother's with Arabella most of the week."

That explains all the stories she's been telling me about her and her grandmother's adventures. She's been talking about it so much that I've found myself wishing I could join them, but I refrain from asking because I know it's not my place as the nanny. Blake's mother seems like an amazing woman though, especially the few times she stopped by when I first started.

"What did you need?" I ask while grabbing my phone form the bench and heading out the barn door, noticing he's alone. "And where's Arabella?"

"She's staying with my mother tonight, a sleepover, which is what brings me down here," he says, shoving his hands into his jean pockets. "Get dressed, we're going to do something."

"Do I get a hint as to what we are doing?"

He shakes his head. "Not a chance."

I roll my eyes, then stop at the front door of the guesthouse. "Any suggestions on what to wear?" I'm nervous to see where he's taking me, but I also can't deny the spark igniting inside of me at the thought of going anywhere with him that doesn't have to do with work.

"Jeans, t-shirt, and boots."

That combination has my mind running wild with ideas, but I nod and head inside to shower anyway without a complaint. Can I really complain much when I'm getting a free week and have nothing else to do? Here I was, thinking Blake was the one avoiding me, but maybe I've been the one avoiding him.

Feelings aren't new for me, but I only recently got out of my relationship with Sean after being with him for two years, and I'm not sure if what I've been feeling for Blake is genuine or not. I'd hate for Blake to think I'm just using him as a way to get my ex's attention, considering he doesn't know what happened in the first place for me to run away.

Instead of pulling my hair back up, I keep it down and let the small waves frame my face in a way I think most men would appreciate. I wonder what Blake is planning on doing tonight in the first place. It seems awfully late to be going out on the town. Once my makeup is done, I take a deep breath before heading back outside and meeting Blake out on his front porch.

I take a moment to drink in how fine he looks tonight, with his dark hair curled in front of his face, eyes darkened in the most delicious way, and clothes that seem to hug all the muscles I know he has underneath. This is probably a bad idea, but my idiotic choices are exactly what brought me here as his daughter's nanny.

So I let him lead me to the large truck sitting in the driveway, one that I haven't seen much of, and help me into the passenger seat while he walks around to the driver's side. I guess there's a plus side to living on the ranch with him — I don't remember the last time I had to drive my car anywhere because Blake is more than okay with giving me a ride.

Not that I've asked him much, but he's already told me that he would take me out since I don't know the area well. That tidbit of information had me wondering if he was worried I'd end up in a ditch somewhere and my insides heat up slightly. He has no damn business making me feel this way. I try my hardest to keep my reaction cool as he heads out of the driveway, then makes a right for the main district.

I'm confused when he pulls into a bar I haven't been to yet, then he gives me a subtle wink before getting out and walking over to my side. He holds a hand out for me and I grab it hesitantly, then jump to the ground. Is it necessary to have a vehicle so high in the air? Probably not, but that's country boys for you.

There's a steady stream of people coming in and out of the bar, each one looking as though they are running on a high. Blake ignores the twinkling gazes from the women as we walk by, his hand wrapped gently over mine so I don't get lost in the crowd. And I know it's a simple gesture, but I can't help the electricity shooting through my palm and igniting inside of me.

While he orders a soda at the bar, he looks over to me for a drink order and I go for a glass of water. I'm not sure what tonight is going to bring, but I refuse to drink a single drop of alcohol until I know what I've gotten myself into. Some of the crowd disperses as a group of women cut between them, and the corner of the room comes into view.

No. This can't be happening. I snap my head over to Blake and glare at him. "You aren't serious right now."

He chuckles. "Very."

I shake my head. "I'll pass."

Blake brushes my words off and leans closer to me, so close that I can smell the fresh scent rolling off him in waves and it has me inhaling deeply. Before he can question what I'm doing, I quickly lean away from him to put some much-needed distance between us. The last time he and I were in a bar together, things took a hot turn and I'm trying to keep myself from making that move again. He wasn't my boss then, but he is now, and I need to remember that.

———

"Is there a Wrenly in here tonight?" the DJ calls and I pause midair with my drink only inches from my lips. "Wrenly, come on over here!"

Everyone in the crowd starts turning their heads, trying their hardest to figure out who the hell Wrenly is, but I'm stuck in place. Blake reaches over, prying my fingers from the edge of the bar that I was gripping with all my might, and pulls me slowly to my feet. "I won't let you get hurt," he whispers to me, and that's enough to have me following him through the crowd.

As soon as I get right next to the mechanical bull, the crowd around me goes wild and chants my name. I'm fairly certain my cheeks are heating, but with the bright lights shining down on me I can't be too sure. I eye the thing in front of me. It shouldn't be too difficult, right? It's a machine, and I'm sure it has nothing on actual bull riding.

Blake gives me a small smile and a thumbs up when I look over to him, then I swing my leg over the contraption and take a deep breath. I barely finish it before the guy in charge of the bull starts it up, the crowd still chanting my name around me. Judging by the silence after a few minutes, I have a feeling no one has lasted this long on it, and that has a bright smile forming on my face.

When the bull spins in the direction of where Blake is standing, my blood boils at the blonde standing next to him with a flirty smile on her face. That's all it takes for me to go flying off the bull and immediately lifting to my feet, more than ready to tell whoever the lady is about herself. Blake finally turns his attention to me when the crowd goes wild, his eyes widening at the look on my face as I stare back at the two of them.

Chapter 10

Blake

I thought it was a good idea at first, since Arabella wouldn't be home for the night, but I should've known it wouldn't go the way I planned. If there's anything my small town loves it's a celebrity, and I guess I'm as close as it gets to one out here. While watching Wrenly hold her own on the bull far better than I thought she would, a woman asked me for an autograph.

I'm not one to turn down those, my fans mean the world to me, but it was the next request that had me getting increasingly uncomfortable. Apparently, the woman is in town for her friend's bachelorette party and wanted me to meet her at the hotel room they're staying in.

I was never raised as anything other than to treat women with care, which is why I forced myself to smile and tried turning the woman down as gently as possible. I'm almost certain she's about to ask me again, but the wild crowd around us has me looking in the direction of the bull. Wrenly is no longer on it, but standing in the center with her fists clenched at her sides while staring at the woman beside me.

For some reason, this has me smirking slightly before turning back to the woman and telling her to have a good night. When I reach Wrenly's side, she flinches from my touch and stomps over to the bar. This time, she goes for alcohol and downs it in one drink, then asks for another.

At the rate she's going, I'll have to carry her into the guesthouse. "Wrenly, why don't you slow down?"

She scoffs. "I'm pretty sure you have someone else to worry about tonight."

Her gaze falls over my shoulder, her eyes narrowing into thin slits, and I turn to find the woman who approached standing against the wall twenty feet away. Her eyes are burning a hole into me, but I ignore it and put all my attention on Wrenly instead.

Wrenly shakes her head and looks to the dance floor. "I think I'm going to dance, feel free to do whatever you want."

Before I can tell her that what I want is to sit here with her, she's already marching out to the floor and getting in front of another guy. I follow his movements as he brings a hand to her hips, each of them moving in sync with the country bullshit flowing through the speakers. What ever happened to soft country music? Now the genre is full of country rap, and that only has these idiots dancing more provocatively.

Wrenly leans her head back against the stranger, then looks over to me with a small smile. It takes everything in me not to walk over there and haul her body away from him. A hand touches my shoulder, making me jump at the contact, but my anger only intensifies when I see it's the same woman as earlier.

She smiles down at me, her fingers grazing over my arm as if she has the right to touch me, and I pull away from her. Her chuckle grates on my nerves. "No need to pull away, sweetie, I'm sure I can make you feel good."

When she tries to inch her hand down my chest, I quickly stand with a glare aimed in her direction. "I already told you no the polite way. I'd rather not be rude this time around. Please don't touch me."

Her bottom lip juts out and she flutters her eyelashes, as if those simple acts would make me change my mind. I shake my head, then walk away from her and head straight toward Wrenly.

Wrenly's movements come to a complete stop when I stand in front of her, my gaze searing into hers. "We're leaving," I snap, then walk away from her and shove the entrance door open angrily. It only takes a couple more minutes before she's following me outside, hands on her distracting hips, and her plump lips set into a thin line.

I shake my head. This is the last thing I need. "Well, get in the truck," I say, waving my hand over to the large vehicle sitting in the parking lot.

She snorts, then crosses her arms over her chest, and I have to fight myself not to look at the curve of her breasts poking out from the V neckline. "Is that how you talk to all the girls? Can't imagine why you're single."

This conversation is going to take a turn I'd rather not go down, so instead of answering her, I head over to the driver's side and climb into the truck. I'm very close to punching the shit out of the steering wheel, but that would require Wrenly to ask questions I don't want to answer. I'm sick of not being able to go out somewhere without a woman thinking she can touch me in any way she wants to, it's sickening.

As soon as Wrenly is in the car and buckles herself in, I peel out of the lot and head the opposite direction of my house. I'm not sure what I'm doing, but I can't bring myself to stop and turn around. This is the last place I want to take someone, but I need to more than ever right now since my mind isn't right. If only Wrenly didn't dance with some random asshole and that woman didn't touch me, I'd be perfectly fine right now.

But I'm one more smart remark from blowing the hell up and there's a place I like going to when I need to calm down and I'm not home to hit the punching bag. Wrenly sighs dramatically beside me, her arms still crossed over her chest in the same way they were outside the bar, and I try to keep my eyes focused on the road.

"Thought we were going home," Wrenly mutters, more to herself than me, but I can still hear her and it has me gripping the wheel.

"In a few, I need to make a stop." Not that I need to explain to her what I'm doing, considering this is my car, but at least she knows we'll be going home soon. I pull onto the dirt path ahead, and follow it until it leads out onto a great big field. "You can stay in here if you want, just give me a minute."

She sits up, eyes wandering over the large space in front of us, and turns her gaze over to me. "Is this the part where you kill me and hide the body?"

I chuckle. "You really have some imagination, huh?"

"What is this place?"

"Just somewhere I like to chill out from time to time, I've been coming here for years." It's a large field, where no lights take away from the stars in the sky. Just ahead of us are large mountains that look breathtaking during sunset — it's one of my favorite times to come here if I can manage it.

The only other person I've brought here was Arabella, and now Wrenly. She still hasn't made a move to get out of the truck, so I lie back

70

on the grass and stare up at the clear sky twinkling with the stars. Even though the car door shutting echoes through the space, I keep my gaze trained up ahead until I feel Wrenly take a seat next to me in the grass.

"You come here a lot?" she asks quietly.

I lean up, taking the chance of looking at her, and immediately regret it. She's not even looking at me. Instead, she has her knees pulled up to her chest and eyes on the sky, exactly the way I did, and I can't move them back. All I can stare at is the way her face looks as she casts her eyes over the vast array of twinkling lights, and the way her mouth parts at the beauty of it.

"Uh," I say, clearing my throat. "Yeah."

She nods, then takes a deep breath before smiling softly. "It's beautiful."

Still, my gaze doesn't move away from her face even as I nod and say, "Yes, it is," in response. This was a big mistake. We should've gone straight to the ranch, both of us stomping into our separate houses, but I just had to take a detour.

"What made you come out here?"

I shrug. "Nothing, really. I was riding around in the truck and noticed the dirt trail, and I've been coming here ever since."

Wrenly nods, then closes her eyes and rests her head against her knees.

"We can head back, I just needed to clear my head." I'm sure she's tired and that would give me the perfect reason to get the hell out of here before I do something I regret.

"No, that's okay. It's nice." Her body somehow angles closer to mine and I slowly sit up. She glances over at me with a frown. "What did you need to clear your head about?"

I lick my lips, wanting to tell her everything I've been feeling with her around, but not wanting to scare her off. "Uh, just that woman at the bar." Obviously, I go for the less consequential option.

"Looked like you were enjoying it," Wrenly mutters, her fingers reaching down to the grass and pulling at the tiny blades. I'm not sure who owns this land, but they've never gotten angry when I'm here. I assume someone owns it, since it's always cut and taken care of.

"Not at all, I hate when people come up to me like I'm a piece of meat."

She hums in response, but stays silent as she looks ahead of us. Even though it's dark, the light from the moon casts a dim glow on the mountain peaks. Something about the awestruck look in her eyes has me bringing my hand to her cheek and pulling her face over to me.

Her mouth parts with a gasp and I'm bringing my lips down to hers without thinking about it. She immediately deepens the kiss, falling back onto the soft ground, and I follow right along with her. There's a bulge in my jeans as I rock my hips against her, loving the feel of her on me, and I bring my lips to the delicate line of her throat.

Wrenly angles her head back, giving me better access, and I take it without hesitation. An owl hoots somewhere in the distance, bringing me back to what's happening, and I pull away quickly. Wrenly is breathing deeply, her eyes narrowed in on me, and I can't even blame her. This is the second time I've made a move on her, only to retract it moments later.

"Uh, I think we should head back to the house."

She nods, wrapping her arms around herself and heading quickly over to the truck without stealing a glance over at me. I adjust myself in my jeans, then head over to my side and hop inside before reversing from the field. It only takes a few minutes to pull up to the ranch and Wrenly is out before I can apologize for tonight, opening and shutting her door without saying a word.

I screwed up this time.

She's the damn nanny, I shouldn't be kissing her, or touching her for that matter. Hell, she plainly admitted she's running away from her ex and my response is to make moves on her? I shake my head, then rush through the front door.

I'll keep my hands to myself from now on.

Chapter 11

Wrenly

Livid.

That's the only way to describe the way I'm feeling right now as I kick the front door to the guesthouse shut. Granted, the anger doesn't stop me from watching Blake's form from the window as he marches up the steps and heads into the main house. My fist tightens around the curtain and I tug it down without even thinking. I blackout from there, rush into each room, throw something against the wall, and watch it shatter into a million pieces.

Even though I'll likely regret it in five minutes, there's a huge weight that lifts from my shoulders at each impact. I hold my breath as I step across the floor, trying my hardest not to get glass in my feet, and fall onto the bed as soon as I get into the bedroom. The exertion from throwing things has my eyes falling closed as soon as my head hits the pillow.

There's a loud knock on the door, forcing me to jump awake and hurry through the living room. My breath hitches when a sharp pain rolls through my foot, and my eyes fall on the mess lying around the house. Before I can even attempt to get the glass impaled in my foot, the knock gets louder on the door and I blow out a rough breath while swinging the door open.

Blake eyes me curiously with his head cocked to the side. "You okay?"

I'm definitely not now that he's standing in front of me. I'm fine with the glass stuck in my skin, but not fine at all with the man standing in front of me. How can he be so nonchalant about what happened last night, or what happened the night in the barn? I give him a curt nod, leaning too much on my right side and only pushing the glass further into my foot.

His eyebrows scrunch in concern and he inches toward me. "Are you sure?" That's when his eyes fall onto the mess behind me and his gaze narrows on me. "So, this is what you do? I give you a place to stay and you decide to trash it?"

Blake pushes closer to me, making me stumble and I gasp at the increasing pain. I'm pretty sure if this thing goes any further in my foot, I'm going to pass out or end up needing to go to the hospital. He comes to an alarming halt, his gaze falling over the broken glass, then coming back to me and drifting to my foot.

"You're bleeding, Wrenly."

I glance down, see a puddle of blood sitting under my foot, and my body sways slightly from the realization of how bad it is. When Blake tries coming closer to me, I shoot him a glare. "No, I don't need your help." While he stays in place, I walk over to the kitchen table and sit in one of the wooden chairs, then lift my foot up from the floor.

I'm not the best with blood and seeing so much of it has my vision blurring, but I blink the haziness away and try to focus on the glass sticking in my foot. The floorboards creaking under Blake's steps have me snapping my head up to him, or rather slowly lifting it, since I'm getting a little queasy right now.

His gaze drops to the foot I'm holding in my hand and he doesn't bother listening to my demand of not wanting his help as he rushes over to me. I try to pull my foot away from him, but he only clamps a hand around my ankle and keeps me in place. "Wrenly, you need to calm down. That's not going to help." He glances around the spot where the glass sits, the piece thick and almost completely embedded inside my foot, and sucks in a breath.

"What?" I ask softly, my voice not able to come out as more than a whisper.

"You might need stitches," he states, glancing at the rest of the mess and shaking his head. "I'm taking the damage out of your pay."

I nod. "I assumed so." Before I can even blink he's got one arm situated under my legs, while bringing the other around my waist, and carries me outside. "Just take the damn thing out!"

"I am not risking you losing too much blood if I do that," he snaps while pulling the car door open and placing me on the passenger seat. "Just don't press down on your foot."

I roll my eyes when he shuts the door, even though my body is feeling too weak for the action, and mutter, "You don't say."

When he gets into the car, he frowns at me. "I heard that." He calls his mother via Bluetooth, letting her know what's going on, then hangs up to focus on the road in front of us. The longer I sit here without getting help, the more blood that leaves my body, and I'm definitely feeling it by the time we pull up to the hospital.

"Hey!" Blake calls to one of the paramedics walking out the emergency room door. "We need someone over here with a wheelchair."

As soon as he gets their attention, he pulls open the passenger door and lifts me from the seat, then waits patiently as they grab a wheelchair for me.

"What's the problem?" a younger male asks while rushing over ahead of the woman with the wheelchair.

Blake points down at my foot, which currently looks like I painted it red, and says, "Piece of glass embedded in her foot." He sets me down gently in the chair, then continues talking to the paramedic and gives him a rundown of what's happening. I slowly nod in and out of consciousness, barely registering when the paramedics start rolling me through the emergency room.

Blake sticks to my side, nervously glancing at his phone every few minutes, and I place my hand on his arm to get his attention. He flinches away from the contact and I give him a small smile. "Head back home, get Arabella on your way. I'll be fine here on my own until I need to be picked up." He starts to shake his head, but I narrow my eyes at him. "Get home, Blake. And thank you."

I order the paramedics not to let him inside with me, then wait for them to wheel me into a room where a doctor is already waiting for me. He takes a look at the glass, then nods. "Alright, Wrenly, I'm going to pull this sucker out, okay?"

"Do I need stitches?"

He gives me a reassuring smile. "I'll know more once we get it out, but judging by this I'm thinking you won't need more than a little glue."

I nod, then take a deep breath when he moves his hand closer to my foot and pulls the glass out. "Shit!" I'm biting the inside of my cheek, blood pouring into my mouth from it, and chuckle. "Sorry."

The doctor chuckles too, then drops the blood-covered glass into the aluminum bowl next to the bed. "No worries, it's a common reaction." He reaches over onto the counter and grabs the glue, then brings it to my foot. "This will be quick, then we can get you all bandaged up and out of here. Sound good?"

I sigh. "Glorious."

———

Blake sticks to my side while I make my way toward the front door of the guest house, Arabella not far behind him. "Are you still going to be able to come with us?" she asks.

I smile at her. "Of course, I will!" Not only am I ready to see Blake back in action, but I love spending time with Arabella and I haven't had much of that since we got back from the last stop.

My eyebrows shoot up when I step into the house, noting the glass that's cleaned up from the floor, and look over to Blake. "You didn't have to worry about that, it was my mess to clean up."

He shakes his head and points at me. "It's bad enough you managed to convince me to let you come with us still, but you aren't supposed to do too much while you heal."

I nod, then turn my gaze away from his penetrating stare. After leaving the hospital, I vowed to myself that I would keep my distance from him as much as possible. That starts now. "Well, I'd like some rest," I say, then watch Arabella frown."But, I'm all yours once I wake up, sweetie." She smiles brightly, then gives me a quick hug before skipping out of the house.

Blake runs a hand through his hair and sighs. "You sure you're okay alone?"

I roll my eyes. "I stepped on glass, boss, nothing major. I'm good, get out of here." I'm trying to joke, but I really need him to get away. After his little saving act, I'm having a hard time keeping my feelings in check. Or non-feelings, I'm not really sure what this is right now.

He chuckles, then gives me a salute before ushering himself out of the house and shutting the door softly behind him. I breathe a sigh of relief, then limp across the living room and into the bedroom. A nap sounds amazing right now after all the pain and blood loss. I guess Blake got that mess cleaned up as well, considering I didn't see a speck of dried blood on the floor when I got inside.

My eyes are falling shut just as my phone blares from the night-stand. I groan and blindly reach for it, then bring it in front of my face to see who's calling me. Imagine that, Sean's name is on the screen. Instead of answering, I silence the ringer, throw my phone on the other side of the bed, and let sleep take me over.

The sun's starting to come down when I peel my eyes open, alerting me that it's probably close to dinner time, and I push myself up from the bed. I make my way to the main house and knock lightly on the door, and almost lose my breath when Blake answers it, as if I didn't know he would be the one to do so in the first place.

"Good nap?" he asks with a smirk on his face.

I chuckle. "Apparently. Anything good to eat tonight? Guess I slept a little too late to make my own food."

"Sure, come in," he says, then steps aside to let me walk past. I do my best not to brush against him as I scoot by him, but my limp has me almost falling into his chest.

"Sorry," I choke out, then hurry past him and into the kitchen where Arabella already has her face stuffed with whatever Blake made for the night.

She immediately pushes off the stool and comes to hug my legs, nearly knocking me down.

"Bug, a little easy on her, okay?"

I chuckle, then rub the top of her head. "No worries, I always accept your hugs."

Blake reaches up into the cabinet where the plates are and my eyes catch on the smooth patch of skin as his shirt rides up his torso. My mind goes back to the night he kissed me outside the barn, when he was bare-chested and sticky with sweat, and I dart my tongue out over my bottom lip.

No.

I shake my head and let Arabella pull me over to the island, taking a seat beside her while I wait for Blake to bring a plate of the delicious-smelling food over to me. He stares at me longer than necessary and I dart my gaze away from him. I refuse to play a part in whatever game he's playing right now, even if every part of my body is vibrating with the need for him.

Chapter 12

Blake

I'm not sure where the protective side came from earlier this morning when I noticed Wrenly had been hurt. Sure, I was angry about all the things she broke in my guest house, but as soon as I saw the blood dripping from her foot, the anger went out the window. It was replaced by the need to make sure she was okay.

Since she promised Arabella she would hang out with her for a bit today, she went outside to play around the yard with her while I got into the shower. I'm sure that's what has me thinking about her in the first place — the fact that she doesn't need to spend any time with Arabella right now, not while I'm here, and she's doing it anyway.

If there's one thing I've realized this entire time, it's that Arabella loves Wrenly, and I'm not sure how she'll take it when the nanny gig is over. I guess there's always next year, but that's if Wrenly is even still in the area or if she's going to keep dealing with me anymore.

Our kiss last night wasn't something I meant to happen, but I gravitated toward her, and can't deny the spark that filled me up while it was happening. I grab a towel from the clean hamper in my room, then walk into the bathroom with the kiss completely on my mind.

I step under the hot water, with my dick aching for relief, and I can't help but bring my hand to my length. The way she felt underneath me that night only has me pumping faster, and the way she deepened the kiss as soon as it started. My spine is tingling, in a way I'm sure it would if Wrenly were in here right now with me and her hand was the one on me.

My breath hitches as I pick up speed, thinking about Wrenly kneeling in front of me, her brown eyes glued onto mine with her lips parted. I bring my other hand up and slam it into the wall, the sound echoing through the room. The image of Wrenly moving my hand out of the way, replacing it with her own, and setting a punishing rhythm has my vision blacking out.

Moments after the shower, Arabella's laughter fills the upstairs hallway along with Wrenly's right behind her and I hurry to wrap a towel around my waist. I'm about to walk out, see what's going on, until I realize Wrenly shouldn't see me like this.

By the time I get to Arabella's door, Wrenly is already sitting beside her bed with a book in her hand, her sweet voice talking with all the character voices throughout.

I lean against the doorframe, smiling at the image in front of me, then quickly walk away. This isn't what I need to be doing right now. While I'm getting into the whiskey, Wrenly's rough footsteps sound through the house as she limps into the kitchen with me.

"She's out like a light."

I nod, then smile at her. "You didn't have to do that today, you know."

She shakes her head. "I love that little girl, you've done an amazing job raising her, and I'll always want to spend time with her. She's not just a job for me."

The words she speaks have my eyes watering, so I hurry to turn my head before she can notice. "We'll be leaving early in two days, so just make sure you're ready. Are you, uh, sure you'll be able to come along with us?" As much as I love having Arabella with me while traveling for the rodeo, I'd understand if I have to leave her here while Wrenly heals properly.

Wrenly groans. "I'm an adult, Blake, I'll be fine. Arabella and I wouldn't miss it for anything." She limps to the front door and I follow her. "Thank you for cleaning up my mess, and for dinner tonight. Goodnight."

Part of me wants to plant another kiss on her lips, but I have a feeling that's the last thing she wants from me. I wait until she gets into her house, then shut the door and head back into the kitchen to down the last of the whiskey in my glass. It would be smart for me to go right to bed, not steal a glance out my bedroom window, but I've been making terrible choices when it comes to the woman living in my guest house.

I watch closely as Wrenly turns the bedroom light on, then steps up to the bed and sits slowly on the edge of it. Her gaze moves around the room, until it lands out the window and I quickly back away from the curtain. That was all I needed to get my ass into bed. I'm not sure she'd appreciate me snooping on her.

Could I really have another meaningful relationship with someone, without having the thoughts of everything Erica put me through? I'm sure I could, but right now I can't trust that someone else wouldn't do the same thing to me. It wouldn't be fair to another woman if I compared her to the way my ex treated me and kept her at a distance.

Wrenly doesn't deserve my hot and cold act, and I can't help but wonder if that's why she snapped last night. It definitely wasn't like that the day before, when I had the housekeeper sneak in there while Wrenly wasn't in, so what else could've happened for her to do that?

A couple more days before we are back on the road, and I'm not sure how the ride will go. How awkward things will get between us.

There's only one way to find out though, and it has me nervous for what's to come. I don't want things to be weird between us, especially if it's something Arabella might end up picking up on. Guess I can't blame anyone but myself for continuing to make the moves on Wrenly.

———

It's later than I hoped when the three of us walk into the hotel lobby, which requires another shared hotel room, and I come to a halt when I get inside. If there's one thing I never expected while traveling, it was to see Erica here, since she never bothered to travel for me. But, there she is, standing right next to Dennis with a bright smile on her face, and it has my entire face heating up.

"Daddy?" Arabella says softly while tugging on my hand. "What are you doing?"

I smile at her, hoping it's genuine even though it feels anything but. "I'm just admiring the place, Bug, that's all."

Wrenly taps Arabella's shoulder, then points over to the couches sitting on the far side of the room. "Want to go sit down while your dad gets everything situated for our room?" She looks up at me and mouths *everything okay?* All I can do is nod, because I'm afraid of what will come out of my mouth if I speak.

Erica turns, her eyes colliding with mine, and she stumbles as if I'm not supposed to be here. I roll my eyes and gracefully walk past her, while Dennis glares at me from the other side of her.

"Blake, it's so good to see you. You're doing great!"

I'd love to shove what she did to me in her face, but not with Arabella in the vicinity. I give her a small smile, praying it comes off as polite as possible, then turn toward the receptionist who's looking back and forth at our interaction. Considering this is our go-to spot for rodeo days, I'm sure everyone around here has heard plenty about my marriage with Erica, and I'm sure they're eager to get some good gossip.

Well, I won't give it to them.

"Hi, uh, Blake Evans."

I can feel Dennis and Erica's stares in my back and I almost spin around and demand to know what the hell they want, but Wrenly comes over with a smile on her face and wraps her arm around me. "Is the room good?"

Erica stares at Arabella, who's holding Wrenly's hand beside her, before she darts her gaze back up to me and gives me a frown. I'm not sure what she expected when she left the two of us. Did she think that she would be the only woman Arabella would ever know, or get close to? And that's the thing, Arabella isn't even close to the woman who should be her mother.

The only woman Arabella has gotten close to since the divorce is the one who's holding her hand and not letting go. Wrenly could've made it a point to stay in the guest house while there was a break in the rodeo, but she made time for Arabella. It warmed my heart when

Arabella and I would get into the truck in the morning and she couldn't stop talking about Wrenly coming into the house to talk to her.

Her real mother hasn't even been able to do that for her, so Erica doesn't get to be upset about the image of Arabella holding Wrenly's hand. There's no more deserving person for the action than Wrenly, and I'd love to tell Erica exactly that. Instead though, I take the room key from the receptionist and walk past the annoying couple slowly with a limping Wrenly next to me.

I hold the door open for the girls, then usher Arabella into the room we'll be sharing while Wrenly heads into the one across the hall to get her things situated. She didn't need to come up to me like that, but I'm sure she saw the way I was reacting to seeing them and she came to my rescue. How is it that she somehow knows me better than anyone else, or am I just that easy to read?

"Okay, Bug, you ready to lay down? There's a long day tomorrow, and I'm gonna have to head out early."

Arabella bursts with excitement. "Does that mean Wrenly gets to do my hair?"

I bring a hand to my chest, acting like she hurt me with her words, and chuckle. "Wow, kid, you really know how to kick a man down."

She smiles sweetly at me. "Sorry Daddy, she just does *so* good."

Can't really argue there. I know my way around hair after having to do it for Arabella so much, but I guess nothing can really beat a woman's touch. I thread my fingers through her curls and smile at her. "It's okay, Bug, I was messing with you."

She lets me get her into the pajamas we packed, then curls under the blankets and steals a glance out the door. "Do you think Wrenly would read me a story again?"

"Did you bring a book with you?"

Arabella rolls her eyes and says, "Of course."

"I'll go see if she will." If I know my daughter as well as I think I do, I'm willing to bet the book that she's been having Wrenly read over and over to her since the other night is the one she packed. It's not going to be too much longer before Wrenly can read it without even having to open the damn pages.

I find her sitting on the couch, her fingers tucked at the top corner of a book, and clear my throat. "Someone's asking for you," I say with a smile.

She chuckles, then sits her book down and walks past me. It would do me good to stay where I am, not witness what's about to happen right now, but I can't bring myself to stay still. I follow behind her, then sit at the corner of the bed while Wrenly grabs the book Arabella's holding out to her.

"This one again?"

Arabella giggles. "I like the voices you make."

Wrenly sighs, then sits at the edge of the bed with a smile directed at my daughter. There's so much love shining in her gaze, that I have to look away from it and focus on the bare wall ahead of me. That doesn't stop her voice from rolling through me though, and it only has me wishing this is something Arabella could've grown up with.

Why is it that Wrenly has no issue sitting down to read our daughter a book, but it's something that Erica complained about all the time?

Chapter 13

Wrenly

I'm not exactly blind, I know something occurred between Blake and the woman he couldn't stop glaring at, and I plan on figuring out exactly what that is now. As soon as Arabella has fallen asleep, I sit the book down on the nightstand, then carefully lift up from the mattress and head out into the living room. During the book, Blake ended up walking out of the room in a hurry, but that's not my concern right now.

There's a small balcony located just outside the large doors in the sitting room, which is much fancier than what we had before, and I limp my way out there. Blake's eyes are closed, his body so relaxed in one of the chairs that I think he's sleeping, but then he pops one eye open and I jump.

He chuckles, and it's such a beautiful sound that I wish I could hear it all day. "Sorry, you need anything?"

I shake my head, then sit down in the seat next to him and stare out at the city ahead of us. It's definitely not the same as it is in his small town of Iris Springs, that's for sure. No wonder he prefers to be there all the time, there's no way anyone is seeing the stars with all this damn light shining everywhere you turn.

"So, want to talk about it?" I ask, breaking the silence.

He clears his throat and sits up, resting his elbows on his legs. "Talk about what?"

"The woman in the lobby."

"I'd prefer not to," he mumbles while grabbing the drink I didn't see when I first stepped out. The swig he takes has me cringing inwardly and I sigh.

"Should you be drinking all that right now?"

He shrugs. "Probably not."

I reach over and grab it from beside him, placing it on the banister beside me, and narrow my eyes at him. "What's going on?"

"That's her."

I arch a brow. "Uh, who?"

"Arabella's mother and my ex-wife."

Damn, and here I was complimenting how beautiful she was. I thought Blake was glaring at her because he was jealous she wasn't standing next to him, the woman is beyond beautiful and I have a feeling she knows it. "Ah, your reaction makes more sense now."

"She didn't even say anything," he states softly, running a hand through his hair. "Our daughter was standing right there, and she didn't say a single word to her."

That almost has me jumping from my seat, more than ready to go figure out which room this Erica woman is in and beat the shit out of her. "Did she mention her to you before I came over?" I remember seeing her saying something to him and she was smiling pretty big, so maybe she isn't a completely terrible mother?

He shakes his head. "Nope, just wanted to tell me how great I was doing this year." His hands wrap around the arms of the chair, clutching them tightly, before they loosen. The veins in his arm have my center getting slick, but I shake the sexual thought away. This is not the time to be getting a huge lady boner.

"Bitch," I say quietly, but not quietly enough that he doesn't hear because his laugh echoes through the night. "Oops, you weren't supposed to hear that."

He smiles, but doesn't bring his gaze to mine and stares straight ahead. "No, I feel the same way, one hundred percent, but what would Arabella think of me if I always badmouthed her mother?"

First, this man had to go and be the most amazing dad, and now he's worried about Arabella seeing him differently if he spoke wrong about the woman who birthed her? I don't care what anyone says, you aren't a mother just because you gave birth. You have to be there for your child through thick and thin, and as far as I can tell, Erica hasn't been there through everything.

If Arabella gets a fever, Blake is the one to come rushing to her side and care for her. Erica would still be stuck to that dumb cowboy's side without even worrying about what's going on with her daughter. How could someone create such a beautiful soul, then walk away as if it means nothing? It baffles me more than it probably should, but I already know I've grown way more attached to Arabella than I should be.

I refuse to let that little girl down by leaving though.

"I think the way you go about things is admirable," I say, part of me wishing I could say the same to my own father. Throughout this entire situation, the only message I've received from him is asking me to hear Sean out. No way in hell is *that* happening. Meanwhile, my mother has only been silent — and somehow, that's even worse.

In a way, I guess I can relate to Arabella on the mom front, and that's probably why I've grown so attached to her. That still makes this entire job much harder to do, because eventually it will be time for me to leave, and what will I do then? I have no home to go to, so where will my next stop be?

"Hey, where did you go over there?" Blake asks, snapping me out of my thoughts. His gaze is on me now, full of concern, and I only shake my head. He nods, then stands from the chair and stretches his arms out. "Well, I'm about to call it a night. Need to get some rest."

I fiddle with my fingers while chewing on the inside of my cheek, which is still raw from the chewing I gave it while in the hospital, then look up at him. "Would you want to watch a movie?"

He tips his head up, thinking hard about the question, then nods. "Sure, but don't be surprised if I don't make it through the entire thing without falling asleep. I'm beat."

My smile is automatic as I lift to stand. I was so distracted that the sudden pain from putting pressure on my foot almost makes me stumble forward, but Blake's arm grasps my elbow. "Thanks, and I won't get too mad about it." Nerves are coming on rapidly now; I'm not even sure why I asked him to watch a movie in the first place.

A dark room, with him sitting next to me? This is a recipe for disaster.

While I get Netflix up on the TV, Blake strides into the small kitchenette and rummages through the cabinets. I'm surprised when he produces a pack of popcorn, which he immediately slides into the microwave. When the popping echoes through the room, both of our gazes dart to the open door where Arabella is sleeping, even though I'm fairly certain she's going to sleep through anything tonight.

"Popcorn?" Blake asks, thrusting the bowl into my face while taking a seat on the other end of the couch. This is good, he's sitting a respectable distance away — which means nothing should end up happening.

I nod and he sits the bowl down on the cushion separating us, and that's even better. This means that neither of us can manage to scoot closer to the other while the movie is playing. This will be easy, even if my heart is beating wildly in my chest. If it weren't for the movie playing in the background, I'm sure Blake would be able to hear it beating from all the way over there.

Our fingers brush against each other as we both reach for a handful of popcorn, neither of our eyes focused on the bowl, and I quickly pull my hand away from his. I make a point after that to glance at the bowl every time I want some, double-checking that Blake grabs his hanful before I reach into it.

Maybe this isn't going to be as easy as I thought.

That's how it works for the next ten or fifteen minutes, until the bowl is empty and Blake moves it from between the two of us and sits it on the coffee table. My palms are sweaty now, but I don't lose my focus on the TV even though I'm not hearing a damn word the characters are saying. If I'm being honest, I've barely comprehended a single thing that's happening on the TV since Blake sat down.

My body is vibrating.

Could I not have had this reaction to someone who's more available? When more minutes roll by, I look down to find that my body is situated in the center cushion and much closer to Blake. Instead of bringing attention to myself, I simply relax into the back of the couch and try not to glance over at the man next to me. I'm not sure what the hell is happening, but it's like he's pulling me toward him without even having to touch me.

I'm not so sure I like that.

It's like I can't control myself when I'm around him, and I'm not sure what will happen if I get any closer to him. Judging by the way things have been going this entire time, I'm not counting on him letting it go any further. Would I even let him if he made another move? So far, each move we've made has been started and ended by him. I'm not sure my ego could handle another moment of him pulling away from me, and I don't want anything to affect my work.

The movie is still glowing throughout the room, and I still have no clue what's happening in it. I only chose it because I saw that The Rock was a main character, and I'd watch absolutely anything he's in.

I jump when my arm brushes against Blake's, and I look over to find my side leaning right up against his. He wiggles in his spot but stays put. Since he's fully entranced by the movie, I take a moment to study the side of his face, and the way his throat bobs as he swallows thickly. It would be so easy to lean up and lick the column of his throat, but I snap my gaze away so I don't give in to the temptation.

He lifts the arm against me, letting me fall into his side, then drapes it over my hip. The spot where his fingers touch my skin pebbles with goosebumps and I shiver from it. This only prompts him to pull me closer, his fingers centimeters from touching the curve of my ass and I hold my breath.

This wasn't supposed to happen right now and I'm more than ready for him to pull away, but instead, I feel his fingers thread through my hair that's laying across his chest. I sit completely still, not wanting to take the chance that the moment I move he stops touching me. I'm an idiot.

A few days ago I was livid with him for playing this game with me, and now I'm an idiot for giving right into it *again*. I sit up, trying to get out of his hold, but he tightens his arm around me and I take the chance to look up at him. The breath I was holding finally blows out, but comes right back in when I see his eyes completely focused on me.

He's looking at me in a way I only saw briefly once before, when we were in the barn, and I'm not sure what to do.

Chapter 14

Blake

I shouldn't do this.

But, how can I not when she looks so damn beautiful looking up at me with those lost brown eyes? She's probably worried I'm going to bolt as soon as I realize what's happening, but that's not the case. I'm completely aware right now, and I have been since the moment she walked outside earlier.

The thing is, why would I keep myself away from someone who makes me feel like I can tell her anything? Granted, I still don't know her situation, but I'm sure she'll tell me about it when she's ready. Either way, I don't want anything to come in the way of this connection I seem to have with her.

Would it really be such a bad thing if I kissed her right now?

My head's telling me not to do it, but my heart is screaming over it and begging me to make my move. To stick with the move I make.

I'm not so sure I can ignore my heart any longer. I've watched Wrenly with my daughter for weeks, treating her like I would want any woman to, and there's nothing that could stop me from taking our connection further this time.

Not even Erica.

She starts to turn her head away, but I bring her gaze right back up to mine. "I'm going to kiss you, Wrenly," I whisper to her. "And this time, I'm not going to stop."

This is the only out I'm giving her. If she pulls away from me right now, I'll leave her alone and let her do the job I hired her for. Then send her on her merry way when the time comes even if it will hurt not only me but Arabella. But right now? I need to kiss her like I need the air I breathe.

As soon as Wrenly nods, I slam my lips to hers and she whimpers against my mouth. I pull her onto my lap, her legs straddling me, and dive my tongue into the warmth of her mouth. I'm certain there's no greater feeling than her lips on mine, her body close to mine in a way it was only weeks ago.

There's nothing stopping this moment, not even myself. She grinds her hips against me, eliciting a growl from deep in my throat, and she does it again. I grip the strands of her hair, tilting her head back until her throat is exposed and I drag my tongue down to it. If I had all night, I'd trace every inch of her with my tongue until there was no part left to touch.

She gasps at the contact, bringing her hand to the back of my head and pushing me further into her chest when I reach the curve of her breasts. I don't think there's anything sweeter than the sound of her moans as I pull her shirt down and wrap my mouth around her rosy bud.

Her hands come to the hem of my shirt, something I thought would be necessary if I was going to be surrounded by her, and she tugs up until it's completely over my head. She throws it somewhere in the room, not that I'm paying much attention to where it went. Not when she's in front of me like this, thrusting her hips against me.

My length is rubbing against her, there's no doubt about that as her movements become more rapid and her breathing heavier. Before she can get any further with catching her release, I quickly twist around until she's lying on her back and I'm hovering over her. "Do you know what's better after eating popcorn?"

She cocks her head to the side, then shakes it, clearly interested in where I'm going with this.

I wink at her while my hands grip the waistband of her shorts, the things that have been slowly killing me this entire time. "Something... sweet." Then I'm placing kisses over her stomach as I slide down her body, loving the way she arches her back to get closer to my touch.

Her eyes widen when I flatten my tongue against her center, before they roll into the back of her head as I flick back and forth. It doesn't take long for her release to coat my tongue, and I've never tasted anything sweeter than her in my life. I'm starting to realize that everything sweet in my life involves her — aside from Arabella — and I can't bring myself to regret this moment.

I'm surprised when she sits up abruptly and pulls my pants down, my hard length bobbing in front of her face. Her mouth opens as she pokes her tongue out, making my body jump slightly from the sudden movement, then she pushes her face into me.

I suck in a breath, but pull her away and smile at her. "That's gonna have to wait for another night, Peach."

I lean down, pressing a sloppy kiss to her mouth and she hums at the taste of her on my lips. "Right now, I need to be inside of you."

———

Wrenly's breathing heavily, her head laying on my chest with my arms wrapped around her, and there's a big smile on my face. She's wiggling against me and I chuckle. "Woman, stop moving."

She sighs. "Sorry, I can't get comfy."

I lift her face up until her eyes meet mine and I kiss her forehead. "I think it's time to head to bed, don't you?"

"But you're so warm."

"And I'll be just as warm tomorrow night," I say with a small laugh, then lift her up from on top of me. My pants are lying right in front of the couch, but I can't seem to locate the shirt. "What did you do, throw the shirt out the damn window?"

She bites her lip and smirks at me. "If that means I'll get to continue staring at your chest? Yes."

I shake my head, then pull her up from the couch, my eyes grazing over every square inch of her bare body. Luckily for her, and unfortunately for me, I sat her clothes as neatly as possible on the back of the couch. She grabs the clothes, slips them on quickly, then walks over to one side of the room and reaches for my shirt that's crumbled into a ball on the floor.

She tosses it at my feet, then hurries over to give me a kiss, before happily walking through the hall and into her own room. If I could go in there and sleep with her tonight, I would, but I'm not sure I'm ready to have a conversation with Arabella about whatever this is yet. It would be a big adjustment for her and now isn't the time to bring it up.

Or tomorrow for that matter.

I peek through the small crack in Wrenly's door, chuckling when I see that she's already passed out in the bed with one leg thrown over the comforter. At least I can say I did my job enough that she fell right asleep, not many men can do that. When I get into my room, Arabella's facing the doorway and sleeping peacefully with her hand tucked under her cheek.

She snuggles closer to me instinctively when I get under the blankets and I press her further into my chest. What would the bed look like if I added one more person to the mix?

———

I wake up to the sound of laughter and an empty bed that has me smiling brighter than I ever have in the past. Knowing that Wrenly and Arabella are getting along so well fills me with joy I thought was never going to come in my life. Don't get me wrong, I love the life I live with Arabella, but having Wrenly with us has been an amazing change.

Already, Arabella has changed so much since she came here. Her attitudes have almost completely stopped, except for the ones she lets slip every once in a while, and she's never been so excited for another person's attention. It's like she can tell that Wrenly is one of the good ones, and that only makes me happy about the choice I made last night.

When I get out into the sitting room, Wrenly has Arabella sitting on the floor in front of her while she braids Arabella's hair slowly. Her gaze barely lifts to mine, but she gives me a smile in greeting. I wonder what's going through her head after waking up this morning, but considering the time on the digital clock, I don't really have time to ask her.

"Alright, Bug, I have to head out. Be good for Wrenly."

Arabella sighs. "I'm always good for her, Daddy."

Wrenly chuckles at her answer, but still doesn't look up at me. Does she think I'm going to regret what I did? I mean, I guess it's not a totally wrong reaction considering how I acted before. She just needs reassurance, but I can't give that to her in front of Arabella, not until we have a proper talk about everything that happened last night.

"I love you, Bug, see you in a little while." I bend down to give her a kiss on the forehead, not wanting to mess up what Wrenly's doing. When I look up and catch Wrenly's eyes on me, I give her a wink, then head toward the door. There's a bag of clothes in my car that I'll change into when I get to the stadium, but my manager has already let me know he's there waiting for me now and I'd hate to be even later than I already am.

When I walk through the back entrance of the stadium Jeff sighs. "About damn time you got here!"

I shake my head and chuckle. "Forgot to set my alarm last night. Everything set for tonight?"

He nods, leading me through various hallways before we get to the room where I'm going to get prepared. I throw my small duffel onto the loveseat sitting against the wall, then sink into the cushions and rub the sleep from my eyes. It sucks that I barely had a minute to spare before walking out the hotel door, but watching Wrenly and Arabella come through those stadium doors later will be worth the wait.

Jeff slaps a hand on my back, jerking me from thoughts of Wrenly and the way she writhed against me last night, and sighs. "Dennis is going to be a tough one to beat this year."

Am I really that worried about beating him still? I've spent what little of the time I've been awake with my thoughts on Wrenly and Arabella, rather than my rival, and I'm not so sure my heart is in it anymore. It would be great to get another win under my belt, I'm sure it would make my uncle proud, but do I really need a win to feel accomplished?

———

As I'm standing along the fence, watching as my competitors fight to stay on their own bulls, my gaze tracks over every inch of the crowd. Erica's standing along the edge, standing stiff as a board while watching the action, and I have to laugh at how ridiculous she looks in this setting. She never did like coming to these things, and I see that hasn't changed.

I'm surprised that I don't feel as angry when I look at her. When my eyes land on the two girls I was searching for, my heart thumps loudly in my chest at the sight of Arabella already sitting on Wrenly's shoulders. They're not close, but they're not too far away for me to see the pinch on Wrenly's face as Arabella bounces on top of her.

I knew she shouldn't have come with me this time, not when she's still healing.

"Evans, you're up!" That's enough to have me putting all my attention on the angry bull inside the gate.

Chapter 15

Wrenly

Throughout the week we've gone to a bunch of different cities for the rodeo, but now we finally have a free day in one of them and Blake asked if we want to go to a zoo not far from the hotel.

Arabella is over the moon, obviously, but I can't stop wondering if Blake really wants me to be there or if he's only asking me for the sake of Arabella. I shake the thought away and choose to focus on finding an outfit for a day at the zoo. I'm sure I have comfier clothes somewhere in my duffel bag.

There's laughter echoing through the hall as Blake jokes with Arabella out in the small living room. I can't believe that each time we get to a hotel they only seem to get bigger and better. This one has an entire living room and a pool table situated on the far side of it, and the kitchen is rather large for only a couple nights' stay.

I know how much Blake loves to cook, so I'm wondering if maybe he made this upgrade before we got here. Arabella also has her own room, which was perfect for Blake and me when he fell asleep with me last night. He was able to sneak into the room across the hall before Arabella woke up.

The thought of him having to sneak out only has my mood dropping. Is he ashamed to talk to his daughter about everything? Hell, does he even see anything more than sex with me, or is it just convenient that I'm with him while traveling? I know I shouldn't let the negative thoughts take over, but it's not something I can help, not after everything Sean put me through.

Finding him in bed with another woman, then finding out he's been committing a crime right under my nose, is not the way I want to live my life. I had to get out of that situation before it ruined me, and the only way I thought I could do that was by leaving. Running away, I guess. Although, was it really running away if you ended up where you feel is right for you?

I've never felt so comfortable in one place my entire life, but I feel like I am more myself around Blake and Arabella than I've ever been around anyone else. The rodeo we went to right after the night we slept together, Blake immediately came up to me after and scolded me for putting Arabella on my shoulders while I was hurt.

As much as I loved that he seemed to care, I assumed it was more because he thought I would drop. Arabella was upset when her father told her she couldn't get on my shoulders again until I've healed, but I couldn't blame him for wanting to make sure she's safe. It's become a routine for us, and I didn't want her to think I stopped caring if I didn't do it, even though it was killing me to.

There's a soft knock on my door and it gets pushed open before I can tell whoever it is to come inside. Arabella rushes over to me, wrapping her arms around my waist with a smile. "Are you ready yet?"

Blake clears his throat, the stern dad eyes directed right at Arabella. "Bug, what have I told you before?"

Arabella sighs and glances at me with an apologetic frown, before turning her attention back to Blake. "Not to barge into someone's room."

He nods, then waves his hand outside the door, and she quickly heads out into the hall. When he's sure she's out of earshot, he leans further into the room and glances at my outfit. "Looking good, Peach."

I'm not even sure where the nickname came from, but he's been calling me that in private since our night in the hotel together. My cheeks flame up, then he's shutting the door behind him with a chuckle. It's like he enjoys getting the reaction out of me.

I finally get out into the living room after ten minutes and find Arabella twitching impatiently in the center of the room.

She sighs. "Finally! Come on, Daddy!" Her tiny hand wraps around mine as she tugs me over to the door without even bothering to see if her dad is right behind us.

Blake shakes his head, but smiles at his daughter's enthusiasm as he follows us out the door. When we get to the lobby, Arabella and I wait for Blake to let the receptionist know we'll be back for our bags in a couple hours.

"So, what's your favorite animal?" Arabella asks me as we head across the parking lot.

I tap my chin. "I'd have to say a monkey, they're the cutest little things."

Arabella scrunches her nose. "Yeah, when they're babies. Then they turn ugly, gross!"

Blake chuckles ahead of us, but doesn't put his opinion into the conversation. I look down at her and raise my brows. "What's yours then?"

She lifts her head up high with a big smile, as if she has the best favorite animal in the world, and I know that no matter what she chooses, I'll act like it is. I'd probably even change mine to whatever hers is, I'm that attached to this girl. "Frog."

I stop just as we get to the car. "A frog?"

Her smile is dream-like as she nods. "Yeah, I'm going to kiss a frog one day and turn into a princess. They're magical."

I'm trying my hardest not to laugh and judging by how red Blake's face is when we get to the door he's holding open, I'm willing to bet he is as well. "Magical?"

Arabella nods excitedly. "Yes, I'm going to find my prince one day." At the sound of that, Blake's expression turns serious in a heartbeat, and this time my chuckle escapes. His gaze snaps to mine, but he only shakes his head before checking that Arabella buckled herself in good.

The ride to the zoo is fairly quiet, but it's not an awkward silence, and it has me relaxing in the seat. Arabella shoots up as soon as we pull into the zoo entrance, her eyes looking over every square inch of the place in amazement. It's crazy to think that I've never been to a zoo before because my parents always thought it was barbaric for someone to take their children to one. I can't even deny my own excitement as we pull into a parking space, and that's exactly why I jump out of the car and head straight for Arabella.

Blake looks at me curiously. "Excited?"

I chuckle, suddenly feeling embarrassed. "I've, uh, never been to the zoo before. Might be a teensy bit excited."

105

His eyes widen, but he only nods and waits as I grab Arabella out of the car. When we get to the ticket window, I try handing my card over to pay for my own ticket, but Blake pushes it away and pays for all of us. I glare at his back, which he must sense because he spins around and grants me the most glorious smile.

Is this what days would be like all the time if I never had to leave?

A small part of me hopes that Blake will ask me to stay, but another part doesn't want to give him the chance to break my heart like Sean did. Speaking of Sean, his texts seem to be coming in more urgently, especially after an article came out that showed me with Blake and Arabella at a rodeo show.

Arabella squeals when we reach the lion's den, her mouth opening wide as one of the large animals lets out a big yawn. "He's so big," she says before backing away from the fence and heading over to the next section.

I have to admit, if it wasn't for Arabella getting so excited over all the animals, I'm not so sure I'd be having as good of a time. There's a long line for the penguins, but it's worth the wait as Arabella and I stare in amazement while they swim happily through the water.

In unison, we both look at each other and say, "Penguins." It's amazing how you can decide your new favorite animal with a little girl who isn't your own, and a man you aren't even sure wants you as more than his plaything.

When we exit the penguin exhibit, I steal a glance at Blake and find him staring at me with a loving expression. Loving? No, I wouldn't go that route. Maybe happiness? I'm sure watching me and Arabella throughout this thing has been a lot for him to take in, and it only has me wondering if maybe I'm getting too attached to her. To both of them.

I shake my head, then lead Arabella over to one of the food trucks.

She scarfs down her food faster than any other child I've ever been around and impatiently wiggles in her seat while Blake and I finish the last few bites of our own. "Gosh, you guys are so slow!"

Blake scoffs and shakes his head, but lets Arabella lead him over to the petting zoo. I stand along the outside of the fence, assuming that he wants to do this with Arabella alone, until he walks over and holds out a cup of food for me. "Come on, Peach."

I shake my head and hand it back over to him. "No, you two enjoy it." I'm not really sure my heart can handle getting any closer to the two of them anyway. It's best if I keep my distance right now.

He scrunches his brows. "Are you okay?"

"Just my foot, been walking for a while and want to rest."

"Of course." His finger shoots out and I catch sight of the bench he's pointing at. "Go sit down, we'll be there soon." Then he walks back over to an excited Arabella, while I head to the bench with my head bowed down.

I hated using my injury as an excuse, but I couldn't see any other way of getting out of the feelings I'm having. This day has been more than I thought it would be, and I'm starting to wonder if I should've stayed in the hotel for the day. Until I look up and catch sight of Arabella's bright smile, and all those feelings go out the window. How is it possible for her to bring out all these emotions in me when she's not even mine?

———

It's late when we pull up to the ranch and my gaze burns into the unknown car parked outside the house. When I glance over at Blake, he's got his hands tightened around the steering wheel and pushes on the gas a little more before coming to a screeching stop. The jolt wakes Arabella from her sleep and she rubs her little eyes, glancing around the area.

The woman standing on the porch as if she owns the damn place isn't someone I haven't seen before, and my blood boils slightly with jealousy. Blake sighs and looks back at Arabella, before bringing his gaze to mine. "Could you take her into the house, put her to bed?"

I nod, immediately doing as he asks, and lift a still-sleepy Arabella into my arms. Erica makes a move as if she's going to come say something to me, but Blake catches her attention before she can and I hurry through the front door. Arabella is already asleep before I lay her in bed, and I take a moment to press a soft kiss to the top of her head.

Blake doesn't even look at me as I walk across the lawn over to the guest house, and that somehow makes me feel worse than if he would've introduced me as the nanny.

Chapter 16

Blake

My gaze doesn't move from my ex-wife, not even as Wrenly makes her way across the lawn and into her designated home. I clear my throat and wave my hand ahead of me, ushering Eric inside. I'm not sure what she's doing here, but I'd rather not find out while standing outside where anyone could hear.

Erica's heels click behind me, then I push the front door open and step aside to let her walk in ahead of me. I can't remember the last time she was here, standing in the entryway, staring at everything in amazement as she is right now. This is the house Erica chose with me, to start our family in. Then she left us without a backward glance.

Hell, she has a daughter that she hasn't even bothered to spend time with, as if her leaving means she can't be a mother. I sigh as I drop my keys onto the counter, then turn slowly to stare at her.

There isn't much that's changed about her. She's still got her light brown hair pulled into a tight ponytail, a tight business dress hugging her hips, and her nails are perfectly polished. There's no sight of acne on her skin, most likely covered in makeup, and it has me wondering why she needs to cover up so much.

Wrenly doesn't need to. She lets her blonde hair frame her face, only pulling it up when Arabella asks her to match, and it's mesmerizing. I shake my head at my thoughts, hating that I'm comparing the new nanny to my ex-wife, and lean against the counter.

"What are you doing here, Erica?"

Erica smiles at me in the same way she used to, before she left me for someone else, and walks slowly toward me. She comes to a stop in front of me with her hand extended, but I flinch away from her touch. I glare at her and it only elicits a chuckle from her as she walks over to the fridge, opening it as if it's something she's done all her life.

"I want to talk to you, make an arrangement," she says as she searches through each cabinet until she finds the glasses. As she pours a glass of sweet tea, Arabella's favorite, her shoulders sag forward and she sighs. "I'd like to spend time with Arabella."

I blink in surprise at her request.

She's been gone for a couple years or so, and *now* she wants to act like a mother and spend time with her daughter? I don't buy it. Instead of answering her immediately, I wait until she puts the tea back into the fridge and turns toward me, then I narrow my eyes. "Spend time with her?"

Erica nods slowly while taking a long sip of her drink. There's a gleam in her eyes that I'm sure would've worked with me before, but it does nothing to me now. What the hell is she playing at? I cross my arms over my chest. "And what's the occasion?"

"Why does there have to be an occasion?" she asks while placing the glass back on the counter. "I haven't been the best mother." Try barely a mother at all. "But, I want to change that."

I arch a brow. "Just like that?"

She shrugs. "What, I can have a change of heart." Her gaze travels the length of my body as she sinks her teeth into her bottom lip. "Can't I, Blake?" When her hand comes to my chest, thankfully covered by fabric, I growl at the touch and wrap my hand around her wrist.

"No, you can't. Where's your new husband anyway?"

Erica waves a hand at me, as if it's a stupid question, and shakes her head. "He's home, safe and sound in bed, while I'm out on a business trip."

I curl my lip at her and chuckle. "Business trip, huh?" My gaze darts around the house, taking everything in, then I force myself to take a deep breath. "Maybe you should come back another time. Now isn't good for me, or for Arabella." Before she can protest, I lead her out of the kitchen and back to the front door, then wave her out of it with a smile.

Her mouth is parted in surprise and she shakes her head. "What are you doing?"

"Well, you said you wanted to spend time with Arabella and she's currently in bed asleep. I suggest you come back tomorrow morning."

She nods, still taken aback by my response, then stumbles down the steps and into her shiny new car. I shut the door louder than I meant to, then walk back into the kitchen and slam my hand down onto the counter. So, this is what she thinks she can do?

Erica thinks she can walk in and out of my life and what, I'll just keep welcoming her with open arms? Maybe I would have done that a month ago, but I'm no longer pining over what happened. She chose the life she wanted, so why is she coming around now?

I'm not stupid enough to believe she actually wanted to spend time with our daughter, especially when she's never made a move to do so before. Not even on birthdays — no card or present, not even popping in. But now, after all this time, she's coming by late at night to spend time with her?

I shake my head and walk over to the counter where Erica's cup sits, still halfway filled with tea, and dump it down the drain. My mind goes back to the look on Wrenly's face when we pulled up to the house and I rub a hand over my face. She looked defeated at the sight of Erica standing on my front porch, barely even looking at me as I asked her to get Arabella into bed.

Part of me wants to walk out the door and make sure Wrenly knows that the woman means nothing to me, but the other part of me knows it shouldn't matter. That's what drives me to head upstairs and into my room, rather than walk across the yard and knock on Wrenly's door.

When I get into the dark room, my feet lead me to the window that looks out at the guest house, and I take note of the darkened house below. Of course she's sleeping. It's been a long few days and she was probably exhausted. So it's a good thing I never went knocking on her door.

Guess we'll see what tomorrow holds.

———

I'm flipping pancakes on the stove when the doorbell echoes through the house, a sound I haven't heard in a while, and I reluctantly make my way to the front door. Erica's standing there, eyes glued to her phone with a frown, while my gaze trails over to Wrenly's temporary home.

Wrenly walks out of her house, until she looks up from the ground and locks eyes on Erica standing in front of me. Instead of coming inside for breakfast like I'm sure she was planning on doing, she turns right back around and disappears through the door. The sound of the wood cracking against the frame from the force of it shutting has Erica jumping slightly and bringing her attention back to the present.

I glare at her. "Erica, didn't expect to see you this morning."

She chuckles. "I told you I wanted to spend time with Arabella, and you said to come back in the morning. So, that's what I did." Her gaze lands over my shoulder, then she brings it back to me expectantly. "Gonna let me come inside?"

"Sure," I mutter, then step aside to let her walk past. Her body brushes against mine, which was completely unnecessary since I'm one hundred percent positive I left enough room for her to get through. "Have a seat, pancakes are almost done."

Her lips curl. "Pancakes? Our daughter needs a balanced diet, not all that sugar." Then she walks through the house as if she's done it for years and disappears into the pantry. "Here, she'll eat this," she says from inside the pantry before walking back out with a container of oats in her hand.

"Erica, she's a child."

She huffs in irritation and shakes her head. "She's going to look ridiculous if she keeps eating all that sugar, trust me."

Is it necessary to let her spend time with Arabella? As soon as I let the thought out, Arabella comes walking into the kitchen slowly while rubbing the sleep from her eyes. "Morning, Daddy." When her eyes land on Erica sitting at the table, she comes to a halt in front of her and blinks a few times. "Mom?"

Erica smiles as if this is the most normal thing in the world. "Hi there, sweetie." She crouches down in front of our daughter and pats her head like a puppy, which only causes Arabella to growl at her. The smile on Erica's face vanishes and she glares at me. "You couldn't have made sure she had a better attitude?"

Gee, I wonder where she got it from. I roll my eyes at her, then turn to continue flipping the pancakes. My spine stiffens when Erica comes next to me and lets out a rough sigh with a shake of her head. "I'll make the oats."

"Or you could go sit down and let me finish the pancakes."

"And let our daughter consume that fattening garbage?" She turns to study Arabella and waves a hand at her. "I mean, look at her, she's had enough of the sugar. It's time to change her diet."

It takes everything in me not to kick her out of the house, but I don't want to hurt Arabella's feelings. I'd hate for Arabella to blame me for her mother not coming around, so I keep my fists clenched at my sides while I turn back to my task on the stove.

Erica smiles proudly at the oats she made and shoves a bowl in front of Arabella's face. Arabella looks from the bowl to her mother and shakes her head. "Those aren't pancakes."

Erica smiles, even though her left eye twitches much like it does when her patience is too thin. "It's much better than pancakes, sweetie."

Arabella pushes the bowl back to Erica with a frown. "I want pancakes."

I smile at my favorite girl and slide her pancakes over to her, knocking the other garbage to the side, then reach for the syrup sitting in the middle of the island. "One stack of pancakes, for a very special girl," I tell Arabella with a wink.

"Thank you, Daddy."

Erica claps her hands excitedly and says, "How about we go shopping for the day? Let your mom pick out some new clothes for you?"

Arabella nods with a small smile, but I've been around long enough that I know it's not genuine. Erica, on the other hand, takes it as true happiness and thinks nothing of it, and that only makes me angry. Angry that she thinks she can come back into our lives in the blink of an eye and expect everything to be the way she wants it to be.

Just as I help get Arabella's shoes tied, Erica walks up to us and stands entirely too close for my liking. I help Arabella up from the couch and make sure to take a few steps away from Erica in the process, then hold my arms out. Arabella wraps her tiny arms around my neck and gives me a small peck on the cheek, one of my favorite things in the world, and smiles brightly at me.

"Be careful," I warn Erica as she leads Arabella out the door. What could possibly go wrong while they're out today? I have no real reason to worry, other than the fact Erica hasn't done much for her since she was born. This was a bad idea, but considering her car is already reaching the end of the drive, it's a little too late to change my mind.

Chapter 17

Wrenly

I'm rinsing out the bowl I used for cereal when there's a hard knock on my door and my body stiffens when I open it for Blake. He smiles at me then looks back at the driveway, which is devoid of Erica's car, and says, "You can have a free day today, Arabella went out with her mother."

There's something off about his tone, but it's not my job to worry about how he's feeling. I nod with my own smile, but it's not as bright as I'd like it to be. There's something wrong with me, especially knowing that Blake has been communicating with a Goddess.

Even if he saw me as more than a nanny, I don't stand a chance against a woman who looks like that.

"Okay, that gives me some time to explore the town." There's an awkward silence as he stands there, staring at me, and I clear my throat. "I'm going to get dressed and head out. Have a good day." As soon as I shut the door in his face, I shake my head and curse at myself for acting so stupid around him.

There aren't many people walking around as I get into the heart of the town, which is fine by me — I'm not particularly in the mood to talk to any strangers today. Ever since I saw Erica, I've been in a weird mood, and I'm not ready to see where that mood will take me.

There's a small boutique around the corner from where I parked the car and I take a chance to head inside. A young woman at the counter gives me a smile of acknowledgment, then goes back to whatever she's working on while I wander around the small shop.

When I get to the other end of the store, there's a bulletin board with different events tacked onto it, and I scan them briefly. One catches my eye and I smile softly — looks like it's coming up this weekend, and I know exactly what I'm going to buy today.

I walk up to the counter and take a deep breath. "Hi, could you tell me the best place for me to get a dress for a little girl for that event coming up?"

She nods excitedly and writes down the name of a store on a blank sheet of paper before handing it over to me. "Let them know Maci sent you over!" Then she goes back to her work, while I walk happily out of the store.

This is going to be such a fun idea, and I can't wait to see Arabella and Blake's reactions when I tell them what they're doing this weekend. I'm going to have such a fun time doing Arabella's hair and making her look even more beautiful than she already is. I get a little turned around, but after asking a stranger which way the store is, I'm finally walking through the doors.

My eyes wander over the different racks of dresses, each with their own flare to them, and I smile. Arabella would look amazing in any of these, but I think I'll end up going with pink or purple — or maybe yellow.

While sifting through the dresses, an older woman walks up to me with a soft smile and waves at me. "Hello. Can I help you with anything?"

I shake my head and give her a polite smile of my own. "Not at the moment. Maci wanted me to let you know she sent me to you. I'm looking for something for the event coming up this weekend."

The older woman's smile brightens and she nods. "Well, you came to the right place. Just let me know if you need anything, hon."

After spending ten minutes looking at the different dresses and none of them calling to me, I almost give up, until my eyes catch on to a dark blue dress hidden beneath the others. As soon as I pull it out, I smile brightly at the image of Arabella walking downstairs in this and I hug it to my chest.

Within minutes, I'm thanking the older woman and walking out of the store with a neatly wrapped box in my hand. I can't wait to see Arabella's reaction when she opens this later, along with Blake's at what rests inside with it. It's weird, I have a free day today and the only thing that brightened my mood was thoughts of Arabella.

I blow out a rough breath when I get back into my car, then pull out of the parking space and head back toward Blake's ranch. I've barely been gone an hour, so I'm surprised when I pull in front of the house and see Blake running around the yard with a squealing Arabella.

They turn their attention to me when I step out of my car and shut the door, but quickly go back to their antics. I take a moment to watch them, smiling at the carefree look on Blake's face as he chases his daughter. There's a warmth spreading through me that has me shaking my head and I quickly make my way across the yard.

I steal one more glance at the two of them before disappearing into the comfort of the guesthouse. Part of me wants to run out there and join them in all the fun, but I'm not sure that would be appropriate. So, instead, I flip the TV on and lounge on the couch until I find a rerun of Friends.

I'm about to doze off when there's a soft knock on the door. I'm surprised to find Arabella standing outside the door, a smile on her face, and she points to where her dad stands twenty feet away. "Come play with us, Wrenly!"

Her happiness is infectious.

I smile brightly at her and crouch down until I'm eye level with her. "You sure?"

She nods frantically. "Yes!" Before I can respond, she's skipping away from my house and back over to her dad who's watching me curiously. Even from here I can see his chest rising and falling with each ragged breath he takes, clearly exhausted from the exercise he's getting.

It's a free day for me, so it would do me good to sit back and relax — not come outside to play with Blake and Arabella. I'm not here to play with them. But, I've never been one to make good choices, which is why I'm slipping my shoes on and rushing out the door to join them.

Arabella claps excitedly, then rushes up to me and grabs my hand. There's a small swing set situated in the middle of the yard that she leads me to, then she takes a seat in one of the swings with a smile. "Push me, Wrenly."

Blake clears his throat and gives Arabella a stern frown. I'm not sure anything is as attractive as him showing his fatherly side.

"Sorry. Can you please push me on the swing?" Arabella asks with her head bowed to the ground.

I nod. "Better hold tight."

As soon as I push her high into the air, she lets out a delighted squeal, but it does nothing to hide Blake's body coming closer to mine. He's standing right next to me as I push Arabella higher and higher, and sighs. "More important things came up," Blake states, his gaze pointed to Arabella with a frown on his face.

"What do you mean?"

"Her mother. Barely had her an hour and brought her back, letting me know she had to take care of work things." He shakes his head and growls. "I never should've let her in."

I take a break from pushing Arabella and turn to Blake, placing my hand on his arm softly, then give him a small smile. "Don't beat yourself up over it, you did the right thing." As much as I hate the thought of it, I admire him giving Erica another chance to be a mother. It's more than most people would do in a situation like his.

His gaze darts down to my hand and I quickly pull it away. "Plus, it seems like she's doing okay."

"Yeah, I guess it could be worse." He runs a hand through his hair before he takes over pushing her. When I try to move away from him, his hand wraps around my elbow to stop me and he gives me a short nod. "Thank you, for trying to make me feel better."

His touch vibrates through me in the best way and I shake from his grasp with a nod of my own. "Of course." Instead of standing here and letting thoughts of BLake run rampant through my head, I let out a fake yawn and smile. "Looks like I'm ready for a nap."

Arabella frowns, then tries to open her mouth to say something, but it closes as soon as Blake clears his throat. She only nods before letting Blake continue to push her on the swing.

As soon as I shut the door behind me, I slide down onto the floor and take a deep breath. I'm not sure what the hell is coming over me, but this isn't what I signed up for. I didn't sign up to crave Blake's touch, or to look at him as if he's the only man in the world.

This time, I really yawn and I head into the small bedroom to curl under the blankets. Maybe a nap will do me good. My window is cracked slightly, so I can clearly hear the squeals of Arabella as she and her dad continue playing together outside. And weirdly enough, my eyes fall shut at the sound.

———

Maybe I should've thought more about this.

I'm staring at the wrapped box that I bought earlier, suddenly nervous at what Blake will think about me buying something like this for his daughter. This isn't my job, it's his. He should be the one buying her things like this, and what if he gets angry that I did such a thing?

I shake my head and take a deep breath.

It won't do me any good to stand here and worry about it, considering it's already been bought. If he ends up getting angry about it, I'll handle it like a champ. The thought of him getting mad has me clenching my thighs together and I shake my head. Is there any time when I don't think of how hot that man is?

My gaze snags onto the clock hanging on the wall and I straighten my shoulders. Dinner is probably ready by now and I'm hoping he'll be okay with me showing up, especially when I have something to give Arabella. I bring my hands over the light-colored sundress I'm wearing and I can't help but laugh at myself.

Here I am, dressed like this is a date, when Arabella's mother has been showing up. What the hell is wrong with me? I shake my head and almost turn back into the room to change my clothes, but I don't have time for that. This will have to do.

Before I can chicken out, I grab the wrapped gift and quickly exit the guesthouse with my hands shaking nervously. I take the steps slowly, my gaze cast down on my feet, until I take the final step onto the porch. My knuckles tap against the door and I hold my breath until Blake swings the door open, blinking at me in surprise.

"Have room for one more?" I ask with a nervous chuckle.

Chapter 18

Blake

There's something about the way Wrenly has been acting this entire time that has rendered me unable to take my eyes off her. She seems nervous, fidgeting in her seat every few minutes, and now that our plates are all cleared, her eyes are darting around the table. I'm about to ask her if everything is okay when she reaches beside her and smiles at Arabella.

"I got something for you while I was out today," Wrenly says softly.

Arabella's eyes grow wide and she smiles brightly. Meanwhile, my heart is beating rapidly in my chest at the idea Wrenly had a day to herself today and she still chose to think about Arabella. She could've gotten anything she wanted for herself, yet she bought something for my daughter instead.

Wrenly pushes the wrapped box over to Arabella and steals a nervous glance at me. It makes sense now, she's been nervous that I'd react poorly to her present. I give her a smile of reassurance that seems to appease her because her spine loosens before she turns her attention back to Arabella.

I have to chuckle at Arabella's frantic movements as she tears at the wrapping paper. The room falls silent at the sight of what's in the box and Wrenly clears her throat, looking over to me. "There's a, uh, father-daughter ball coming up this weekend. I thought you two might want to go together."

She not only thought of Arabella while she was out, but me as well, and that has my heart stuttering. What the hell is going on?

"Can we go, Daddy, please?" Arabella's high-pitched question has me snapping from my thoughts and I give her a smile.

There's nothing going on this weekend, so why not spend it at a dance with my favorite girl? "Of course, Bug." I nudge my head toward Wrenly's silent form. "What do you say?"

Arabella snaps her head to Wrenly and smiles at her. "Thank you, Wrenly, I love it!" She hugs the dress to her chest, proving her statement right, then jumps from the chair. "Can you help me put it on?"

Wrenly chuckles and nods. "I guess we can see how good it fits, since I wasn't sure of your size." Then she looks over to me. "As long as your dad says it's okay."

"Don't let me stop you," I say with a smile.

I watch as the two of them rush up the steps excitedly and I can't stop my mind from wandering into dangerous territory. After all, this is something that I should've expected from Erica, not the nanny. Instead, Erica chose to bring Arabella back after barely spending any time with her, while Wrenly bought Arabella a gift.

It's got my body warming at the thought, wanting more than anything to slam my lips to Wrenly's even if it's a bad idea. I shouldn't be thinking like this, not about my daughter's nanny, but how can I not? Their giggles can be heard all the way downstairs, and it's a sound I rarely hear from my daughter around anyone but me.

When they come back downstairs, Arabella gushes over the dress and how pretty it is, while I lead her back upstairs to get ready for bed. I have a smile on my face when I get downstairs, but it quickly falls when there's no sign of Wrenly. It's probably for the best, I'm not sure what I would've done if she was still here.

All morning, I heard nothing but excitement from Arabella as she went on and on about the dance. Now I'm standing in front of the mirror in my room, fixing the tux I pulled from my closet, with a smile permanently etched on my face. I'd do this every single day if it meant my little girl was as happy as she is right now.

And it's all thanks to Wrenly. Had she not gone out, I never would've thought to take Arabella to this dance. I'm surprised she didn't focus on herself for the day, but that's not something I want to spend more time thinking about. I've done nothing but think about it since she gave the dress to Arabella.

It doesn't help that Wrenly is currently in Arabella's room with her, getting her all dolled up for a night out with me. Wrenly could be doing anything since Arabella and I will be gone for a few hours, but she's helping my daughter instead. I could've easily paid for someone to come over and do Arabella's hair and Wrenly insisted that she would love nothing more than to get Arabella ready.

According to her, that's one of the things she was looking forward to the most. Part of me wonders what Wrenly will think of me in this suit, while another, smaller, part of me knows wondering is wrong. It seems that with each day Wrenly is around my walls keep crumbling down.

Erica hasn't gotten back in touch with me about Arabella, which doesn't really surprise me, and thankfully Arabella hasn't had a chance to think too much about it. All I've ever wanted is for my little girl to have both her parents in her life, but it seems like that wasn't in the cards for her. That's okay though, I can do the job of both parents.

Wrenly had asked if she could take Arabella out earlier today to get her nails and toes done, which I was more than happy to approve. Seeing that someone else wants to dote on my little girl fills me with a happiness I haven't felt in a long while. A happiness that I thought was gone ever since Erica walked away from us. It's slowly starting to creep back in though and I can't help but realize it's because of Wrenly.

I've spent most of my life being the one to laugh and smile with Arabella, I haven't realized that she may need someone else to do that with. Someone like Wrenly. I shake my head and take a deep breath. Now isn't the time to get into that thought, not when my little girl is right down the hall getting prepared for a night out with me.

The suit I'm wearing is a little tighter than it used to be, but it will have to do for the night since it's the only one that will go with the dark blue of Arabella's dress. I guess I'll need to go out and get some new tuxes, just in case.

God, I'm pathetic right now.

Here I am, done and ready to walk outside my room, but I'm stalling the time by thinking about any and everything I can. I have no doubt that Wrenly will make Arabella look like an absolute princess, which is something that's worrying me. I don't know if I'm ready to see my little girl looking grown up.

I'll admit, I never would've imagined that Wrenly was this good with kids — considering her limited background with children — but she's done an amazing job thus far. She's never treated Arabella as anything less because of her age, and I admire that about her. I'm still curious as to what happened between her and that ex of hers, but I'm sure she'll tell me about it when she's ready to. I've got to be patient until then though.

I glance at the tie I'm wearing and shake my head. Maybe I could go with a different color, rather than something as simple as black. There's a rack on the back of my closet door where all my ties are hung and I study them carefully. Blue is one of my favorite colors, so I have plenty of blue ties, but which one would look best with Arabella's dress is the real question.

After a few minutes of staring at the blue ties, I finally reach for one and get rid of the black. When I get back in front of the mirror, I feel a little better than I did minutes ago and nod to myself. I've got this.

When I get out into the hall, I smile at the sound of giggles coming from Arabella's room and quietly walk past the door. I'm glad that Arabella has a woman to talk to, at least for the time being, until I no longer need Wrenly here. The thought of Wrenly leaving has my chest aching, but I push the feeling away and focus on standing at the bottom of the steps.

Or sitting.

I'm not sure when Arabella will be ready, but I want her to feel as important as she really is to me and that means I'll meet her at the bottom of the staircase. Exactly like in the movies. My palms are sweating and I wipe them on my leg, no clue as to why I'm so nervous — it's just a father/daughter date night, what could possibly go wrong?

While waiting, I steal a glance out the front window and notice the large carriage waiting outside the house. Wrenly said that she had a big surprise for Arabella, but I never would've imagined this to be it. She's really going all out for this night and it only makes my walls tumble down further.

If they come down any more, I'm not sure what will happen.

The floorboards creak above me as the girls walk around the room and I quickly spin around and head back to the bottom of the stairs. Arabella should be ready soon, especially if she wants to get to the ball on time. I look at the watch on my wrist, noting that we only have about ten more minutes before we need to leave, then focus my gaze on the top of the stairs.

I take a deep breath when Arabella's door opens and plaster a big smile on my face, but Wrenly is the only one who comes rushing out of the room. She gives me a small smile as she scurries down the steps, gets a drink from the kitchen, then goes right back up to Arabella's room.

What could possibly be taking them so long?

I've been staring straight ahead for so long that the throat clearing at the top of the steps has me jumping in my spot. My eyes widen as I watch my little girl slowly descend the stairs, a big smile on her face, and the most beautiful gown covering her body.

The hand I have behind my back makes an appearance, where I'm holding a bouquet of Arabella's favorite flowers and I extend them out to her. "You look beautiful, Bug."

Arabella shakes her head with a chuckle. "You have to say that, Daddy!"

I give her my arm in hopes she'll take it, then start for the door, but the sound of Wrenly calling for us has me halting my movements.

Her breaths are ragged as she steps close to me and says, "Uh, pictures?" She cocks her head to the side and something about the movement has me wanting to step closer to her, claiming her lips as my own. But, I keep myself in check.

"Of course," I say softly as I lead Arabella over to one of the plain walls and wrap a long arm around her. As I stare into Wrenly's gaze behind the camera, all I can see is the heated look in her eyes — one that I can't seem to ignore, no matter how hard I try.

Before my thoughts can get some action, I clear my throat after a couple pictures and nudge Arabella's shoulder. "Ready to go?"

Arabella nods enthusiastically, while Wrenly smiles lovingly at her. How is it possible that she seems to love this little girl more than her own mother? It only makes my attraction for Wrenly that much deeper, and all I can do is lead Arabella out of the house, right toward the carriage that Wrenly ordered for us.

Chapter 19

Wrenly

My breath is still caught in my throat as I watch Blake and Arabella ride away in the carriage, thinking how unreal it is how good he can look in a suit. As soon as I walked to the top of the steps with Arabella, I couldn't help but let my gaze travel down his broad form. I could tell that the suit was a little tight on him, but that only made my mouth water more.

The dark gray suit is nothing like I've ever seen on him, even the day I came for the interview when he wore a black suit. I thought black was his color, but tonight proved me wrong.

And the way he had his hair slicked back, just for a night out with Arabella, nearly sent me to my knees. I bring my phone to my face and scroll through the pictures I took of the two of them and smile to myself. I've never felt such a peace like I do when I'm around the two of them.

A text message comes through from my ex and I roll my eyes, sliding the message from view and ignoring it. Here's to hoping he'll realize I'm not going to respond and finally leave me alone — not counting on it though. Instead of worrying about the text message, I click the lock button on my phone and walk through the empty house.

They'll be gone for a few hours, at least, and now I'm sitting in here alone with nothing to do. I don't like it. I fidget in my spot and head into the guesthouse to get some of my clothes into the wash, then head into the bedroom and take my bikini out of a drawer.

Blake has a heated pool and it's about time I make use of it while I'm here alone. I slip the bikini on, then head out to the pool. I grab a beach towel from the pool house and lay it out on one of the beach chairs. The cool air feels nice against my skin and I breathe in the fresh air before diving into the warm water.

While I float on my back, my mind conjures an image of Blake joining me and slowly making his way over to me. His fingers brush over my flat stomach until they reach the flesh popping out of the top. My breath hitches at the fantasy running through my mind while heat flows through to my core.

I've never felt anything as hot as the flame coursing through me at just a simple thought. He's touched me before and I know exactly what it feels like, so it's not hard to imagine what his fingers would feel like on me right now. Each touch to my skin would send a shock-wave rolling through me, making my legs tremble from the simple touch.

I take a deep breath and walk through the water, then jump out and head over to the chair where I laid out my towel. There are bright pink and yellow flowers on it, with a blue background, and I'm trying my hardest to let the images of those flowers shake my thoughts away. It doesn't seem to be working though.

All I can imagine is Blake jumping right out with me and wrapping his arm around my waist, while pressing his lips to the sensitive spot on my neck. If he were actually here, he'd spin me around and trail his lips down my collarbone and over the curve of my breasts.

I'd let him push me back onto the towel as he continued to trail his lips downward and stop just at the waistband of my bikini bottoms. I take a ragged breath and skate my hand down the length of my body, then push my fingers under the fabric of the bottoms I'm wearing.

This is what I would encourage him to do, and he'd have no problem with doing it. His thick fingers would run over me, making my body tremble, and I'd spread my legs wide for him — giving him the invitation he desperately needs, that I desperately need.

Is this what it's come to?

I'm sitting here alone and all I can do is conjure up images of him doing these things to me? It's pathetic really. He's out, probably having the time of his life with Arabella, and I'm sitting along the pool with my fingers brushing over my aching center.

I blow out a rough breath and rip my hand out from under my bikini bottoms, then stomp away from the pool. The cold air is hitting against my body in the best way, releasing some of the heat that's taken residence inside me, until I swing my front door open and walk inside.

Should it really be this hard not to think about him?

All I wanted to do was swim, but I can't go anywhere without fantasizing about the things he could do to me. I shake my head at myself and walk into the kitchen, where a small wine cabinet sits, then grab whatever bottle my fingers grasp onto.

As soon as I pour a small glass, I'm tipping the contents down my throat and sighing contently into the empty room. This is what I needed, a little bit of alcohol to get through the night. To get through the thoughts running through my mind.

After I pour another glass and down that, I pour one more and head back out to the pool. There's a small wooden stand situated next to the chair I'm taking up, so I sit my glass down and turn back toward the rippling water. There are lights situated throughout, blinking in different colors, and I watch them change in fascination.

How have I not come out here before?

I mean, it's a pretty decent set-up he has back here, and I'm just now taking advantage of it. It's a travesty, really. Now that my mind is blurred from the alcohol, I do exactly as I did when I first got out here and dive into the pool. When I pop out from under the water, my gaze catches onto the bright red numbers on the digital clock, showing that it's been at least an hour since Blake and Arabella left.

How can one man have so many clocks lying around?

Why would you need a clock next to the pool?

I shake my head and exert myself by doing a few laps until my arms are burning from the exercise, then I go back to floating above the water. As I float around the pool, my gaze snags onto a mountain of pool equipment and I smirk at the bright orange lounge raft situated on top.

The perfect thing to lay out in the pool with.

My nipples perk at the rush of air as I rush over to the orange raft, then hurry back to the pool with it clutched in my hand. I plop it onto the water and situate myself on top of it before kicking the edge of the pool. Once I'm safely in the middle of the water, slowly moving around with the waves from my kick, I shut my eyes and listen to the hum in the air.

The cold air mixed with the warmth coming up from the water creates the perfect pair and I curl into it. I remember the glass of wine I brought out with me and groan at the idea of me not bringing it in with me — I need to drown myself in it before I drown myself in thoughts of Blake some more.

God, I just can't get my mind away from him.

When I drift over to one side of the pool, I poke my foot out and keep the raft still before hopping off. I quickly grab the glass of wine and head back onto the raft, kicking away from the edge just as I did the first time. Now that I have the wine with me and I'm floating on a cocoon of warmth, this has finally turned into the perfect night alone.

————

I jolt at the sound of creaking in the distance, my arms flailing above me, and catch myself before I tip into the water. When I twist my head around and peak over the back of the raft, Blake's figure is standing just under the pool lights and he's staring right at me.

Instead of the tux he had on earlier, he's now sporting a pair of swim trunks. That's it. There's no shirt to hide the six-pack, and his hair has since been tossed in front of his face. He shakes it from his eyes while smirking at me, then drops into the water with me.

This is a bad idea.

A terribly bad one.

His form comes closer to me and I try to move away from him, which is obviously a failure since I'm currently on this stupid orange raft. When he gets as close as he can get, I flinch back and fall right into the water. Sure, the water is warm, but it's nothing compared to the heat coming from his touch as he wraps an arm around me to lift me from the water.

He chuckles, the sound vibrating through me. "You good? I didn't mean to scare you or anything."

I shake my head and let out a nervous chuckle of my own, which only comes out as a snort and I mentally smack myself in the head for it. "No, uh, it's fine. Your pool and all." Then I wave to the raft and sigh. "If I was tired I probably should've gone back inside."

He nods, then glances around the space, before bringing his gaze back to me. "It is pretty relaxing out here."

I awkwardly glance around the pool, then blow out a rough breath. "How was the, uh, dance?"

His smile brightens against the darkness encasing the pool. "It was amazing, and I forgot I never thanked you for it."

"Oh, no, you don't have to do that."

Blake inches closer to me, that bright smile still on his face, and nods. "I do, Wrenly. We never would've done this tonight if you didn't kickstart it."

My cheeks heat at the compliment and I turn my gaze away from him. "Well, as much as I'd like to continue this conversation, I'm going to head back inside for bed." I chuckle at the statement. "Like I should've done before."

I slip when I try to lift myself out of the pool, which only has Blake place his hands on my bare skin to help me up, and I have to close my eyes at the heat coming from them. When I'm finally on the pavement, I take a deep breath and pluck the towel from the beach chair.

Blake clears his throat from the pool and I find him wiggling the empty wine glass in his hand with a smirk. I might not be right in front of him, but I know there's a dimple poking out on his right cheek. "Forgetting something?"

My chuckle is rough as I hurry over to him. "Seems so." I grab it from his hand, my breath catching when our fingers brush over each other, and pull away from him slowly. The heat in his eyes is very dangerous right now and the only reason I back away from him.

I quickly push the front door to my temporary home open, then shut it softly behind me and lean against it. The heat in his eyes is something I'll never be able to get out of my head and it's only going to drive me more wild for him.

Chapter 20

Blake

I fling my head back against the edge of the pool and groan into the empty night. My hands were so close to gripping her, putting my lips to her soft and glistening skin, but I managed to refrain from doing that. But now? Once she turned around and sashayed her hips away from me, my eyes couldn't help but follow the movement.

I'm not sure if she meant to catch my attention, but she did regardless. It seems as though that's all she's managed to do since walking into my life the first night in the bar. She's done nothing but stay in my head, from the brown eyes to the softness of her skin. It's all still programmed into my head.

I take a little bit to run laps from one end of the pool to the other before finally lifting myself out of the water and scrubbing a towel through my hair. When I walk through the back door, I head right to the small bar sitting in the corner of the game room and pour myself a long-awaited drink.

The liquid burns down my throat, but not nearly as much as my fingertips burned when they made contact with Wrenly's skin. How is it possible for one human to affect someone so profoundly? I shake my head at the question and place my empty glass back on the counter, then head out of the room and upstairs.

Maybe if I get some sleep my head will be back on right in the morning. At least, that's what one could hope. Instead though, I run back through my night with Arabella and smile at the images running in my head.

She had the time of her life, the happiest I've ever seen her, as I spun her around the dance floor with all the other fathers and daughters. There was another little girl there that Arabella is friends with from school and they kept gushing over each other's dresses.

It's something I'll want to do with her again, for sure. For now though? I think I'm going to make it a weekly thing where I take her out somewhere, maybe even take her to get her nails done. That's another thing she wouldn't stop talking about the three hours we were gone — how good her nails looked.

I wonder if that's something she'd rather do with another girl though — someone like Wrenly. Guess I won't know if I don't try. When are you supposed to get your nails done anyway? Is it like hair and you have to wait a certain period to go back?

These questions lead me to bring my laptop out and I lean back against the headboard of the bed, going down the rabbit hole of researching nails. I never thought I'd be up late researching things like this, but I guess this is what happens when you have a daughter.

It seems as though you should keep up with nails at least once a month, maybe less if you're only polishing them. I'll have to talk to Wrenly in the morning and get her input on it. If there's anything I've noticed most about her it's that she loves talking about Arabella.

Could it be so easy to have found someone who finds the same joy in kids that I do? I shake my head and blow out a rough breath. This is stupid. Wrenly is the nanny. It's entirely unprofessional to see her as anything more.

But didn't you already see her as more when you slept with her?

That little tidbit of information always seems to come back to me. The way she arched her body into mine, silently begging me for more, to touch her in a way she's never been touched before. I slam the laptop shut and throw myself onto the other side of my bed, a side that could easily be occupied by the petite woman staying in the small house below mine.

It just doesn't stop.

No matter what I do, or don't do, Wrenly seems to always worm her way into my head. I try to shake thoughts of her away, but it's no use. Once they start, there's no way to stop them, no matter how hard I try. She's everything I've always wanted in a woman, but this is the feeling I've done nothing but run away from ever since Erica left.

How could I possibly give my all to someone else, just for them to stomp on my heart? It's not something I'm willing to go through again, which is why I've kept myself locked up tightly with only Arabella... seems like that's working out for me now, huh? It's like Wrenly cast this spell on me and I can't seem to get myself out of it.

She could be thirty feet away, yet I'm still able to know when she's in the same room as me. Even when I'm not looking. There's this charge in the air whenever she's around, a force that calls to me, and I always try my hardest not to turn and stare until she's made herself known. This isn't something I've felt with anyone before, not even Erica, and I'm not sure what to do about it.

Do I ignore it, or do I run with it and hope for the best?

My head is telling me to stay as far away from her as possible, while my heart is screaming at me to give her the chance she deserves. But, does she see me like that?

I chuckle softly to myself. Obviously she did see me like that, considering the night she spent with me after the bar, but now that I'm her boss? I'm not so sure.

What if this is strictly professional for her? After all, that's exactly what I told her this would be once I realized who she was. But I've done nothing but have unprofessional thoughts about her since I saw her and I don't think I can hold myself back much longer from taking action.

Listen to me, I sound like a lunatic.

I shake my head at myself and lean over to shut the lamp off on the nightstand, bathing the room in darkness. With my window open, the only sound piercing through the air is crickets and the hum coming from the pool. It's soothing and has my eyes dropping closed quickly.

Arabella is giggling when I walk into the kitchen, with Wrenly sitting on the other side of her with a bright smile on her face. I give them a small nod in acknowledgment, then head toward the coffee maker for a cup of coffee. A warning to anyone around me — you don't want to mess with me in the morning before I've had my fill of caffeine; it is not a pretty sight.

When I turn towards the two girls, they're leaning into each other, their eyes casting over to me before jumping into a fit of giggles. I'm not so sure I like where this is going right now.

I clear my throat and arch a brow at the two of them once they look over at me. "Something funny?"

Arabella shakes her head, but there's still a smirk on her face. Wrenly nudges into my daughter, pointing amused daggers at her face to keep her quiet, then turns back to me. "Nope, nothing at all."

They can't seem to stop staring at my face, but I choose to ignore it and get started on breakfast. "Pancakes again?"

"We already ate breakfast, Daddy," Arabella says cheerfully from her seat.

Looks like I'll be eating on my own today. "Any plans for the day?" I ask Wrenly.

She looks down at Arabella, then gives me a small smile. "I was actually wondering if I could take Arabella out to town with me, maybe do some shopping if that's okay with you."

Just knowing that she wants to take Arabella out, without even really having to do that, makes me want to cross the room and kiss her senseless. But, I'm better than that, and instead nod with a smile. "That sounds fun. Any idea where you'll go?"

Wrenly sighs. "Actually, yes. It seems as though there's a carnival in town, and Arabella seemed super excited to go."

Carnival?

God, I can't remember the last time I went there. I've tried avoiding that place like the plague, since that's one of the first few dates I took Erica on when I met her. So it surprises even myself when I spin around and ask, "Mind if I join you guys?"

Wrenly's eyes widen and she nods. "I don't see why not. You sure you don't want the day to yourself?"

Most parents would love nothing more than to get a break from their kids, but that's not the kind of parent I am. I enjoy doing things with Arabella, but it seems as though with Wrenly here I'm figuring out new things to do with her and I'm not willing to miss those. If I remember the carnival correctly, I'm sure Arabella will have the time of her life.

"I'm sure. When are you guys heading out?"

Wrenly looks over at the clock on the stove and clicks her tongue to the roof of her mouth. "I'd say, maybe an hour? I still have to get ready, and so do the two of you. Should that be enough time?"

I nod and give her a smile. "More than enough." Wrenly lets Arabella know she'll meet her out front in an hour, then rushes out the door to get ready, and silence ensues.

"Isn't Wrenly so pretty?" Arabella asks, stunning me for a moment.

"She is, Bug." I'm not sure where this conversation is going, but please don't let it go where I think it is. I mentally cross my fingers and pray for the best but, as usual, that doesn't do much for me.

"Do you like her?"

I choke on nothing but air at her question and nod my head. "Sure, sweetie, she's done a very good job of taking care of you."

Arabella rolls her eyes and jumps down from her seat. "No, I mean, do you *like like* her?"

"I'm not sure that's appropriate, honey. She's an employee, that would be unprofessional."

"What if she wasn't an employee?"

At that question, I glance over at the clock and groan as if time is running out to get ready — even though only a few minutes have passed since Wrenly walked out the door. "Looks like we need to get you dressed for the day, or else we'll be late." I lead her over to the stairs and open her bedroom door, then sift through the clothes in her closet.

A nice pair of shorts and a frilly tank top seems like a good choice, then I'll get her hair braided back for her after I give her a bath. I'm not sure what I'll wear, but I'll make sure to take my time so Arabella can't come back to this question. My daughter doesn't forget anything, which is a blessing and a curse — specifically for moments like this.

Once I get the shower started for Arabella, I quickly head into my room and try to think about what I could wear. Usually I'd go for anything, but it seems as though my mind is wondering what Wrenly would like to see me in.

Ridiculous.

You can never go wrong with a plain white t-shirt and jeans though.

By the time I finish getting dressed, Arabella is already wearing the outfit I picked out for her and waiting for me to do her hair. The wet strands are soaking through her shirt, so I quickly make my way across her carpeted floor and ease myself onto the bed. There's a stack of rubber bands sitting in the top drawer of her nightstand that I pull out, then place her between my legs as I get to work.

When we get outside, my body stiffens at the sight of Wrenly standing in the driveway with her hands shoved deep in tiny jean shorts. God's testing me, that's the only thing I can think of at this point... and I'm going to fail.

Chapter 21

Wrenly

It's been weeks and today is the big day — the one where Arabella and I watch Blake kick some ass. I stretch from the hotel room bed and head into the bathroom for a quick shower. It's too early for Blake to be gone already, but I'm sure he'll be ready to leave once I get myself ready. I'm full of excitement, but that doesn't mean there aren't nerves hidden deep inside of me.

After watching Blake throughout the weeks, there's one thing I've realized — this is a very dangerous sport. Each time we watch him fight himself to sit upright on a bull, my heart drops to the pit of my stomach, then I'm smiling brightly when he perfects the craft.

No wonder his thighs are so toned.

I sigh as I step under the hot spray of water and run my fingers through the strands of my hair. When I lift my hand away, a few pieces stick to my palm and I roll my eyes. It truly sucks when you shed like a damn dog. The pelting water lands on my hand, sending the pieces of hair onto the shower floor and down the drain.

As soon as I'm done, I step out of the shower and slip my arms through a white robe hanging on the bathroom door. The softness clings to my wet skin and I wrap my arms around myself to snuggle into the fabric. There's a small dresser sitting along the wall with a mirror above it, so I use that as a makeshift vanity to get my hair and makeup done.

When I'm done, I blow out a rough breath at trying so hard, but there's no going back now. I'm stupid for wanting to get Blake's attention in the first place. I grab my wallet sitting on the nightstand and tuck my phone into the pocket of my shorts, then swing the bedroom door open to find Arabella and Blake reclining on the couch.

Blake's attention turns to me and his gaze tracks the length of my body, pausing for a minute or two on my bare legs. He clears his throat before pushing up off the couch and running a hand through his hair, then leans down to give Arabella a soft kiss on the forehead.

I'll never get over how much he dotes on his little girl. Even if you didn't know him and saw him in passing, you can tell the love he has for Arabella. It only makes the heat simmering in my belly that much more eager to be let loose. I shake my head and give him a small smile before rushing into the kitchen for a much-needed cup of caffeine.

My body vibrates with the energy radiating through the room as he makes his way into the small kitchenette and I have to force myself not to turn around. His gaze is burning a hole through me, begging me to bring my gaze to his, but I stay with my back facing him.

Blake clears his throat and groans. "I gotta get over to the stadium, warm up for tonight. You'll be okay with Arabella?"

I'm surprised he's asking, considering the entire reason I'm here is to take care of his daughter in moments like this. Instead of questioning him, I give him a simple nod while mixing the contents of my drink. Still refusing to turn around and face him. No good can come from me staring at him for long periods of time.

When the door finally shuts behind him, I spin around and eye Arabella curled up on the couch with a cartoon on the TV. I bask in the hot liquid scalding my tongue as I take a quick sip of my coffee, nothing feeling better than the warmth coasting through my bloodstream.

"Okay, munchkin, ready to get all dolled up?"

Arabella pokes her head over the couch, then turns her gaze over to the TV before bringing it back to me. "Can I finish this first, please?" Well, when she uses her manners so well, how could I possibly deny her?

I give her a big smile and nod, clutching the warm mug in my hand as I head over to the couch with her. She scoots over a few inches so I can sit beside her and leans on me once I get situated into the thick cushions. My ass is already cramping from the couch digging into it — I'm convinced I'll never get into a hotel that actually has comfortable furniture.

I've been trying to convince myself that it's why I do nothing but toss and turn throughout the nights, even though I know that's a blatant lie. Most nights, I lie awake in bed and think about Blake. I mentally groan and throw my head back against the couch, wishing I could get the attractive man out of my head.

Arabella stands once the cartoon is done, then scurries down the hall and into the room across from mine where she slept. I took advantage of the occasion and told Blake I would pack Arabella's things for this trip, so I know exactly what I'm going to dress her in.

Her eyes are brighter than normal as she watches me take out an outfit that looks almost identical to mine, and she claps her hands excitedly. "This is going to be so much fun!" She tugs the articles of clothing from the bed, then hurries into the adjoined bathroom to slip them on quickly.

When she comes back out, I've already got everything situated on the bed to do her hair. The reason I didn't want to chance a look at Blake was because of the shirt I'm wearing, the one I had made for just this occasion. Blake's last name is printed on the back, with some corny lines about bull riding, and I was nervous to see his reaction to it.

I can't wait for him to see Arabella in her outfit though. Watching his face light up every time he sees her makes me want to steal glances at them every minute of every day. I'm pathetic.

I'm used to tightening Arabella's hair into French braids, but I'm thinking of doing something a little different and curling it. She has the most beautifully soft hair that hangs down her back in waves and I'm willing to bet they would look amazing with tight curls.

She sits in front of me, making herself comfortable, as I twirl the wand through thin strands of her hair. The lowest heat setting for about ten seconds does the trick and I let the curls fall down on her back. It takes about thirty minutes to finish everything up, then I let Arabella walk over to the mirror and inspect everything.

When she turns to me with a bright smile, I know I did good and as I pack up the mess I made. Since the wand is hot, I carry it into the bathroom adjoining my own room and sit it gently on the marble-top sink.

"Ready, beautiful?" I ask, holding my hand out to her in invitation.

She nods excitedly and wraps her tiny fingers around my palm, letting me lead her down the hall and out the hotel room door. Just as promised, there's already a car waiting for us outside that Blake sent to us, and I carefully place Arabella inside before sliding in next to her.

My nerves are going haywire right now, since this time I have to catch Blake's reaction whether I like it or not. I take a deep breath when we pull into the stadium, which is already crowded with guys and girls in cowgirl and cowboy attire. Once Arabella is unbuckled, I clasp my hand with hers tightly as we push through the crowd — which seems to be growing with each second that passes.

Once we get to the front doors, where a security guard eyes us curiously, I give him my name and he ushers us inside. It takes a few wrong turns in the large space before my gaze finds Blake's about thirty feet away. My gaze softens when he flings his head back, laughing at something the large man next to him says, and I find myself slowing my steps.

The slower I go, the longer I have until I have to face him, but it seems as though Arabella has different thoughts. She pulls me eagerly through the dirt-packed area, until we get within a couple feet of Blake who still hasn't noticed us. When the guy talking to him looks over Blake's shoulder, I watch as his eyes peruse down my body and I fidget uncomfortably.

Blake notices the change and spins around, his blue eyes clashing right into me. There's a gleam in them, but it only lasts a split second before he's spinning back around to face his friend and says something I can't hear from this spot. The friend produces an amused grin, then nods and heads off in the opposite direction without looking back.

"Daddy!" Arabella squeals as she rushes over to him and jumps into his arms.

I have to dart my eyes away from staring at his arms as they wrap around her small body, instead focusing my attention on the other men walking around the space. There's a guy leaning against the wall in a dark corner and his gaze lasers in on me, making me feel naked under the stare.

"Wrenly?" Blake says softly. and I jump when his hand falls onto my shoulder. He scrunches his eyebrows in concern with his head cocked to the side. "You okay?"

I chuckle nervously and nod. "Of course. I should be asking you that. This is it!"

He tries to turn his face and cover up the blush creeping up his cheeks from my attention, but he doesn't do it well enough. "Yeah, I guess it is." There's something off about his mood, as if he's not as excited about this moment as he has been since I started working for him. "How about you take Arabella to get something to eat before the place is swarming with people?"

"That's a good idea," I say with a smile, before angling my body toward Arabella. "Hungry?"

She nods, then leans up to give her dad a kiss on the cheek, before letting me lead her over to the open concession stand.

————

I've watched each and every other contestant with my nerves only increasing each minute it gets closer to Blake becoming the center of attention. I've learned some things while coming to each rodeo, and I have a good feeling about Blake's chances of winning, but that doesn't keep my nerves from consuming me.

As soon as they announce Blake's name through the speakers, Arabella looks up at me with a knowing smile. This is our thing now — when it's Blake's turn to shine, I lift Arabella up onto my shoulders so that she can see her dad dominating. It might be scary as hell, but I can't deny the pleasure that builds inside of me every time I watch him out there.

Arabella screeches Blake's name as they let him and the bull out of its cage and I chuckle at her excitement. My hands are shaking slightly and I try to ebb it away by clutching onto Arabella's legs tighter. Not too tight that I hurt her though, enough that I can stall the shaking.

When the eight seconds are up, that's the moment my body loosens and I let out a scream of my own. I listen as the announcer rattles off Blake's score and I know without a doubt Blake did it. He won.

Chapter 22

Blake

I thought I would be jumping for joy after this.

It's what I wanted this entire time, to show up the man my ex-wife left me for and prove that I am better than he is. I've done it now, so why does it feel like something is missing? The crowd cheers around me, but my gaze darts around the stadium to find the only two pairs of eyes that matter right now.

I'm not sure why I've been putting off this attraction. Wrenly is beautiful and adores my daughter in a way I wish Erica would've. A soft hand wraps around my arm and I smile at the touch, but it falls when I spin around and come face to face with Erica.

She's grinning from ear to ear, her hair hanging over her shoulders in a way I'm not entirely used to, but it does nothing for me. There was a time when my heart would race at her smile and I'd do everything in my power to bring it to her face. But now? Her smile isn't the one I want to be witnessing right now.

I want to watch as Arabella and Wrenly hurry through the screaming crowd, then wrap both of them in my arms when they

151

reach me. My gaze skips over Erica and eyes the rest of the crowd, and I frown when I don't catch sight of Wrenly.

Where the hell are they?

Erica squeezes my arm to gain my attention, then angles her body closer to mine. "That was amazing!"

I nod, giving her the best smile I can manage, and slowly ease away from her touch. "I guess so."

She scoffs. "Don't downplay it." I shiver as she brushes her fingers over my arm, uncomfortable with the contact. Her touch isn't the one I want to be feeling right now, not even close, which only has me looking into the crowd once more. Still, nothing.

Erica continues her perusal with her fingers, until she's gripping the collar of my shirt, and she leans up with a smirk. "And you looked incredibly hot out there."

It takes everything in me not to laugh at her words. What do you know? As soon as I win the title her current husband won, she's back on top of me. That only sickens me and I back away from her.

Can't she just leave me alone?

Instead of focusing on the desperate woman in front of me, I keep my eyes peeled for a flash of blonde hair, but that doesn't last very long. In a second, there's a set of lips connecting with mine and my eyes widen at the action. What the hell is she doing? I bring my hands up to her shoulders and push her away, and that's when I feel the energy in the air change.

When I glance up, my eyes connect to Wrenly's brown ones, which are bright with tears threatening to fall down her face. I try to push around Erica, but she tries blocking my path and I glare down at her.

"Erica, we are done. There's nothing between us. Leave me alone, now."

Her mouth parts in surprise as if it isn't possible for someone to deny her, and I quickly step around her. Isn't her husband in the crowd somewhere, stewing over his loss? I can't imagine he'd be too happy knowing his wife just made a move on me.

That's not your problem, Blake. Wrenly is.

When I get to the edge of the crowd, Wrenly is standing with Arabella, then pushes her towards me when I come into view. I open my mouth to holler out her name, but a group of girls bombard me and I lose sight of her in the chaos.

Arabella.

A large body comes next to me, yelling at the greedy fans to back up, and creates an opening in the throng of people. Arabella stands there, her body shaking, and I rush over to her. As soon as she's in my arms, I breathe her in deeply, then place her back on the ground.

"You okay, Bug?"

Arabella nods, then darts her gaze around the stadium. "Where's Wrenly?"

I sigh and run a hand through my hair. "That's a good question. Why don't we try to find her?"

"Okay." Her wide eyes search through the women gathered around the fence, hoping that one of them turns out to be Wrenly, and I hate that my little girl is worried right now.

Why would Wrenly run off like that?

Because you're an idiot. Now's not the time for me to berate myself. I shake my head and focus on the task at hand — finding Wrenly in a sea of people. It's like trying to find a needle in a haystack. Each way I glance there's a blonde that is the same vibrant shade as Wrenly's, but I'd know the shape of her body anywhere.

I pull Arabella with me, until we reach the parking lot outside, the streetlights casting a faint glow onto the pavement. There's a plethora of cars parked throughout and I growl low in my throat, knowing Wrenly is probably hiding behind one of them. If only Erica hadn't pressed her overly glossed lips onto mine.

Who needs that much lipgloss anyway?

Wrenly's are always perfectly natural and pink. Plump without even having to force them to be that way. As soft as what I would assume a cloud feels like. Now I'm thinking about her perfect lips, when I should be looking for her. My hands are clamming up over Arabella's and I look down at her.

She blinks her eyelashes at me and frowns. "I'm tired, Daddy."

I nod and glance around, hoping to catch sight of Wrenly's blonde hair, but there's nothing in sight. "Alright, Bug, let's get you back to the hotel then, okay?" When I turn around to head toward the space where I parked my car, I halt my movements at the sight of Erica standing in front of me. "Not right now, Erica."

Erica shakes her head and glares at me. "This was always the problem with you," she snaps while crossing her arms over her chest. "The reason I had to leave." Her gaze drops to Arabella, but there's no emotion in them, not like there should be.

"*Our* daughter is tired," I grind out and hurry around her small frame. "Go with your husband, I can't imagine he'd be happy about the stunt you pulled tonight."

She shakes her head and wraps her hand around my wrist, keeping me from moving forward. "I don't want to be with him, Blake." Her lips tip at the corners as she looks at Arabella, but there's nothing genuine about it. This is her way of trying to get in my good graces: by using our daughter. "I want to be with the two of you."

I chuckle. "Oh, is that why you've been calling and texting after spending twenty minutes with your daughter?"

She flinches at my words, then scoffs. "I had to work, you know that."

"That's what it always comes down to, right? When are you going to put Arabella above your job, huh?" Arabella yawns beside me and I shake my head. "As I said already, Arabella is tired and I'm taking her back to the hotel." Then I narrow my gaze at her. "Just leave us alone, you've done pretty well at that before."

I don't let her get another word in before I'm stomping away from her and pulling the back door to my car open aggressively. My gaze darts back over my shoulder and I sag in defeat when I still don't see a sign of Wrenly outside. My only hope is that she'll find her way back to the hotel.

Before I get on the road, I lift my phone from my pocket and send a quick text to the driver that drove Wrenly and Arabella here. At least I know someone will keep their eyes out for her while I take Arabella back to the hotel. When we get there, I try to send a text to Wrenly once I tuck Arabella into her bed, and I sigh when it goes unanswered for ten minutes.

Where are you, Wrenly?

I'm tired out and would love nothing more than to lay back on the couch, but my brain is too wired on Wrenly's whereabouts to worry about sleeping. A shower would do me good right now. It will at least pass the time while I wait for Wrenly to get back.

If she gets back. I sigh into the empty space, which feels a lot emptier without Wrenly's presence here. She looked broken when I caught her stare earlier, as if seeing Erica's lips on mine was an arrow straight through her heart, and I feel like a dick.

The cool water feels glorious on my aching muscles as I relax under the spray and I let my mind roam to what Wrenly is feeling right now. She has to feel the same way as I do, why else would she rush out of the stadium like she did? Or seem defeated by Erica's actions?

She probably thinks I'm trying to get back with my ex, but I'm more than ready to tell her she's wrong. I've done nothing but try to get the images of her out of my mind, thinking it was for the best if I didn't act on them, but maybe it's better if I do.

Maybe it's time that I put the whole professional thing to bed and tell her that she makes me crazy. When my muscles are satisfied, I turn the hot water on and clean myself off — nothing is worse than the amount of sweat that pours from your body during the rodeo. I go as quickly as I can, not wanting to miss Wrenly walking through the door, then step out of the shower.

I swipe my hand over the fogged-up mirror and glance at my reflection. The bags sitting underneath my eyes are more than noticeable and also not at the top of my list to worry about. The floor creaks outside the bathroom and I poke my head out, expecting to see Arabella up but instead my eyes clash with Wrenly's dark, bloodshot ones.

She shakes her head and walks over to the bed, flopping into the mattress with a sigh, while I study her body to make sure she's not hurt. I have no clue where she's been. Who knows what happened while she was out there alone? The silence flowing through the room has me inching out of the bathroom with my clothes balled up in my hand and slowly closing the distance between us.

Her eyes fly open when I get within a couple feet of her and she springs up into a sitting position. My heart cracks at the look in her eyes, as if she can't stand to see me standing here, and I reach my hand out to brush my fingers along her wet skin.

Shit, she was crying. All because of me. Well, Erica. "Wrenly," I say softly, hoping she can hear the apology in my tone. My body is itching to be closer to hers.

She shakes her head and curls into the blankets. "I'd like to sleep."

Right. Of course. I quickly walk out of the bathroom and head into the living room, making a bed for myself on the uncomfortable cushions.

Chapter 23

Wrenly

I'm not sure I've ever felt so burned by something as I did when I saw Blake locking lips with Erica. That's why I had to get out of there as quickly as possible. Before he ended up catching on to the fact that my feelings are a lot more than I've let on. That went to shit though when I came into my room to find Blake using my shower.

As soon as he got a good look at me, his jaw clenched tightly at the realization of my hurting. When he said my name last night in a pained whisper, I couldn't bring myself to look at him, not when my mind wouldn't stop running an image of that kiss on repeat. The one that I wish I had experienced with him.

When he was announced as the winner, Arabella and I immediately made our way through the crowd. Unfortunately, we weren't the only ones, and it took a lot longer than necessary to make it over to him. The entire time though, I had been eager to jump into his arms and slam my lips to his.

Thank goodness I didn't make that mistake though.

My head feels like someone whacked me with a sledgehammer and I groan as I lift up from the bed.

This is what you get for spending your night crying like a lovesick fool, Wrenly.

Footsteps outside my door have my head snapping up at attention, eyeing the shadow of feet under the door, until they disappear and the steps fade into nothing. The last thing I need right now is to talk about whatever the hell happened last night. It was stupid of me to think that I'd actually have a chance at something with him.

It doesn't matter how much I love his little girl and see her as practicallymy own, or that I haven't been able to stop thinking about him since the bar. I square my shoulders and take a deep breath, pushing the thoughts out of my head. This isn't something I have to deal with anymore. The rodeo is over and that means he doesn't need my services anymore.

Not for a little while at least.

Yes, that's what I'll do. We'll get back to the ranch, I'll hide away in the guesthouse, then come tomorrow morning I can leave before Blake even wakes up. Before anyone wakes up. My eyes sting from the thought of leaving Arabella, but I have no other choice. If I'm going to get through this heartache I need to go away as soon as possible.

I grab the small backpack from the corner of the room and stuff everything I brought for the trip inside, then step out into the hallway. Blake and Arabella are giggling at each other, neither of them paying attention to my presence in the room, and I take a moment to study them.

Arabella's eyes twinkle with nothing but love for her father, teeth shining brightly in the dim room as she throws her head back with a smile on her face. Blake brings his finger to the tip of her small button nose and pulls away with a laugh. I can't help but crack a smile at the white dot Blake leaves behind and the widened stare Arabella gives him.

"I'm going to get you back," she mutters with her tiny arms crossed over her chest.

Blake chuckles before leaning over with a paper towel and wiping the whipped cream from her skin. I fidget in my spot, causing the floor to creak beneath me, and his gaze snaps over his shoulder to me. He sits straighter in his spot and runs a hand through his dark strands. "Morning," he chokes out.

I nod in acknowledgment, then look over to Arabella with a smile. "Looks like you're having a good morning."

She giggles. "Daddy's silly."

There's a tension in the air as we all stand in silence, so thick you could slice it with a butter knife. Before things could get any more awkward, I turn into the kitchenette and grab my cup from the sink. It's the one I've always used and can't go anywhere without — a Winnie the Pooh one that I got from the Disney store when I took a trip to New York City.

I'm pretty sure if I filled the mug with water it would still taste exactly like a cup of coffee with how much I've drank from it. Once I finish putting the creamer into the cup, I spin around and face Blake with an arched brow. "When are we heading out?" It's best to act casual, like nothing ever occurred last night.

He sighs and looks back at Arabella. "Might sit for a little while, enjoy the morning. That sound good to you?"

I nod and take a long necessary sip of my coffee. If I'm going to be in close proximity to him for the next couple hours here, then in the car for a few hours on the way back to the ranch, I need this caffeine to get through it. "Yep, sounds good." I'd love nothing more than to sit down and enjoy their company, but I'd rather not recap yesterday the entire time.

Alone time is what I need. I can feel his stare on me as I walk away and do my best not to turn around to look back at him. But there's still a pull to him I can't ignore, so I glance at him before disappearing behind the bedroom door. Once the door's shut, I lean against the slab of wood and let out a low groan.

This is going to be torture.

———

We're coasting down the interstate when Blake clears his throat. "Can we, uh, talk?" he asks.

I sigh and turn my head over to him, then look back out the window to watch the cars blurring past. "There's no need to talk."

"I think there is, Wrenly. Please?"

There's a part of me deep inside that wants to give in to him, let everything out into the open, but the bigger part of me knows this can't be any more than it is. I simply shake my head, not bothering to take my stare away from the glass, for fear that if I turn my stare over to him I'll blurt everything I want to say.

Like, how I've felt nothing but safe and at home when I'm around him and Arabella. That my smile has never been as bright as it is when I'm in his presence. The way my heart beats uncontrollably as soon as he walks into the room, and his perfect smile takes my breath away.

I can't tell him that now, not when Erica is in the picture.

The rest of the ride goes by without another word, not even the radio to drown out the deafening silence, until we're finally pulling into the driveway. He lets out a long sigh, then shoves his door open and gestures for Arabella to climb out as well. I watch as the two of them head up the steps, wishing more than anything we could be walking inside hand in hand, big smiles on our faces.

Before I can make a mistake and rush after him, I quickly step out of the car and push open the door to the guest house. The best thing to do is steer clear of him for the rest of the day or else he might sense my plans for the morning. I can pack what few things I brought here with me to pass the time, maybe get it out to my car, that way all I have to do is walk out tomorrow.

It's a good plan and one I get started on right away.

When there's a light knock on my door a few hours later, I hold my breath and stay as still as a statue, hoping that Blake will get the hint and walk away. Maybe he'll think I'm sleeping.

"Just wanted to invite you over for dinner," he says with a sigh before knocking once more. My body is itching to take a few steps to the door, but I force myself to stay strong and frozen in place. After waiting a minute or two, he groans, then says, "Well, I'll see you in the morning I guess."

Or not, I want to mutter. But I'd rather not have to deal with him rejecting me when I know my heart won't be able to handle it. When I'm sure he's a safe distance away from the house, I take a ragged breath and head into the bedroom. I may have been pretending to be asleep, but the exhaustion is starting to take over and it's about to be very real.

I'll shower when I get to whatever place in town to stay. There has to be somewhere here in Iris Springs for me to take residence until I figure my shit out. I'm a runaway, this was the first job of many on my adventure. Thankfully I've been working for Blake though, who's paid me a good chunk and let me live in the guest house rent-free.

So, I've been saving up the money he's paid me, and it should last a little over a month. That's plenty of time to figure out another place to go and a job to get. My breath is shaky as I climb under the blankets and curl them beneath my chin before closing my eyes slowly.

———

There's an ache in my chest that I've been trying to ignore since the other day, but it's vibrant today. Practically burning inside of me as I cast a glance at the large ranch house ahead of me. I really wanted to say goodbye to Arabella, but it will only make my decision that much harder to bear.

My eyes are stinging, begging for me to turn around and go back inside that house, put all my things back where they were, but I can't bring myself to listen to their pleas. I blink rapidly, letting the tears wet my cheeks and fall onto the seat of my car.

With an empty heart and cracked soul, I ease my way down the driveway until I turn onto the backroad leading to Blake's house. I swipe at the tears in my eyes and press on the gas, moving faster down the deserted road. Each meter I get away from Blake's, the harder the tears fall down my face and my vision starts to blur.

Driving right now probably wasn't the best decision, but there was no other way for me to leave unnoticed. Not when everyone on Blake's payroll will tell him anything they think he needs to know. When I get into the heart of town, I find the bed and breakfast situated on a bright corner, across from an ice cream shop that's occupied by the owner.

I walk inside, instantly overwhelmed with the floral scent flowing throughout the space, and smile comfortably. There's an older woman, no younger than seventy, sitting in a wooden chair beside the reception desk with her gaze fixed on a puzzle book in her hand. Her gaze hasn't lifted to mine, so I tap the bell on the counter, and she jumps at the sound.

"Oh, dear, sorry." She shakes her head with a chuckle and smiles at me. "That's what I get for bringing the book out. What can I do for you, hon?"

Give me the strength I need to leave this town. That's not what I tell her though. Instead, I smile and say, "I'd like to book a room for two weeks." Because I'm not entirely sure how long I'll need to be here, but it's better to be safe than sorry.

Chapter 24

Blake

I'm nervous this morning.

My plan is to make breakfast for Arabella and me, then take a plate to Wrenly since she missed dinner yesterday. Or chose to skip it. I'm trying to keep an open mind on the situation though.

When I get downstairs, there's no light on in the kitchen or sign of Arabella in the kitchen waiting for me. She was probably exhausted after the long couple days we've had, so I can understand her need to sleep in some today. I grab a medium-sized glass bowl from the cabinet, then search around the kitchen for everything I need.

Even though Arabella is obsessed with pancakes, I'm thinking we can have something slightly different today. I open the fridge and grab different fruits — strawberries, blueberries, and raspberries — then pull two bananas from the counter. As I carry everything over to the island and sit it down, Arabella walks into the kitchen slowly.

"Sleep good, Bug?"

She nods her response, clearly not up to the task of talking just yet, and I spin around to grab different sauce options for the crepes I'm making. I grab the large jar of peanut butter, Nutella, and marshmallow fluff, then a few things to make a vanilla sauce to put on mine.

Arabella watches me with a tired gaze, her hand resting under her chin as she leans into it. Her eyes follow me around the kitchen, catching my movements as I slice up small pieces of fruit. "What are you making?"

I think of the best way to explain these to her and smile. "They're basically a thin pancake, with fruit and other different things put on top."

She nods in response, clearly okay with the answer, then watches me mix the batter together and heat up a small skillet. It only takes about ten to fifteen minutes to get all the crepes done and I place the serving plate in front of Arabella.

"Get as many as you want, and grab whatever toppings."

It doesn't take more than a couple seconds for her to lean over the island and drop toppings onto her crepes, the tip of her tongue sticking from the corner of her mouth. While she digs into her food, I grab another plate and load it up with a sampling of everything, then head toward the front door. "I'm just going to take a plate over to Wrenly, I'll be right back."

She mumbles something in response as I slip out the front door in my plaid slippers, the most comfortable footwear I own. It's eerily silent as I make my way over to the guest house and there's a sinking feeling in my gut that I'm not sure I like. I tap lightly on the door and frown when I don't hear any shuffling on the other side.

My gaze runs along the driveway, noting that Wrenly's car is no longer parked in it, and I run back into the main house for an extra key. Arabella gives me a nervous glance but doesn't bother questioning me right now, not that I'd want her to anyway. I could be paranoid right now and Wrenly just went out into town for a few things.

When I get back to her door, I take a deep breath before unlocking it and stepping inside. As soon as I cast my gaze around the room, there's something off about the space. I walk through the small living room and poke my head into the bedroom.

My body stiffens as I walk around the room, noting there's not a hint of Wrenly throughout the place. Her things are gone. No sign of her anywhere. When did she leave? It had to have been before I woke up this morning, which means she prepared herself for this. She wanted to make sure I was asleep when she left.

God, how will Arabella react when I tell her Wrenly left? I mean, she had every right to. The job was only until the rodeo ended and she took the chance to leave as soon as we got back. She didn't even say goodbye.

I let my shoulders drop in defeat and head back out of the small house, not ready to face Arabella with the truth.

Arabella is sitting on the couch when I get back inside, the plate I had made for Wrenly still sitting on the island where I dropped it when I grabbed the extra key, and she stares at me for a minute. "Is she sick?"

This is it.

It's going to break her tiny heart and that's the only reason I let anger take over rather than the sadness and hurt I'm feeling. How could she have gotten so close to Arabella and not tell her goodbye? I shake my head and let out a rough sigh, wringing my hands together in front of me as I sit down next to Arabella on the couch.

"Uh, no, Bug, she's not sick."

She nods. "Tired?"

Arabella is a smart girl. If I keep answering her without a straight answer she's going to get suspicious and find out anyway. I shake my head slowly and place my hand gently on her thigh, giving her the best smile I can manage considering things. "No, honey."

"Well, where is she?" Her head perks up, hoping that Wrenly walks through the door, and it only makes me get angrier.

"She left, Arabella."

Arabella's head turns to me and she cocks her head to the side. "Left? Like, for a little bit?"

I run a hand over my face, absolutely hating that I have to tell her this, and give her thigh a squeeze. "No, for good." Maybe once Arabella goes to bed I'll try to search through the house to make sure Wrenly didn't leave a note, but I'm not counting too much on that.

The moment her eyes water, I wrap my arms around her and let her cry on my shoulder. Unfortunately, the moment doesn't last long when there's a rapid knock on the door. I've barely lifted from the couch when the knock sounds again. *Someone's impatient.*

Part of me hopes it's Wrenly coming to change her mind about leaving, while another part of me knows she's not coming back. When I swing the door open my irritation increases tenfold at the sight of Erica standing on my porch.

"What are you doing here?" I ask as I cross my arms over my chest.

She smiles brightly, as if this is the most normal thing in the world, then lunges at me. "I'm coming back!"

She's what now? I push her away from me and narrow my eyes at her. "Uh, I'm not sure that's what we agreed on. Pretty sure I asked you to leave us alone."

Erica chuckles and pushes at my chest playfully. "Oh, you didn't mean that."

I really don't have time for her shit right now. "I did, and you shouldn't be here right now." Not when Arabella is upset and I have a feeling Erica won't be sympathetic toward her about it.

Instead of listening to me, she pushes past and rushes into the house with her eyes falling right onto our daughter with tears falling down her face. I've never seen Arabella cry like this before, they won't stop coming down — it's like a waterfall. "Erica," I mumble, following her through the entryway and into the living room.

She stands tall in front of Arabella with her hands on her hips and her head cocked to the side. "What's wrong?" There's no hint of care in her voice as she asks the question, and it has me more than ready to defend her if necessary.

"Wrenly left this morning," I say quietly, not giving Arabella the chance to speak.

Erica's eyes narrow on Arabella and she shakes her head. "Well, there's no need to be upset about that, I'm here now." The way she says it has every part of my body tensing up now that I know the real reason why she's here now. "Your mother," she grinds out with a fake smile.

She's threatened by Wrenly.

"Erica," I say with a hint of warning in my voice.

Her gaze comes to mine and she gives me a small smile. "Yeah?"

"She's allowed to be upset."

"Why should she be? The woman was only the nanny, no one important."

The idea that she could talk so horribly about someone she doesn't even know, someone I've grown to care deeply for, has me clenching my fists at my side. I open my mouth to say something to her, but Arabella lets out a tiny growl.

"Don't talk about her like that!"

Erica's lips curl up before she schools the feature and clenches her jaw. She takes a deep breath with her gaze locked in on Arabella and bends down to her level. "You shouldn't speak to your mother that way."

Arabella doesn't look away from her mother's stare as she says, "And you shouldn't speak about Wrenly that way." My little girl's a trooper, that's for sure.

Erica lifts back up and wipes her hands on the pencil skirt she's wearing, then points a finger to the stairs. "Go to your room. You'll come out when I say you can."

"Erica," I snap. "She's hurting, leave her alone."

Erica scoffs and shakes her head. "Thank goodness I came here, or else you would let her walk around like she owns the place." Then she turns her attention back to Arabella and arches a perfectly shaded brow, no doubt painted on with makeup. "Go."

Arabella's entire body shakes as she rushes past Erica and up the steps.

"That was completely unnecessary," I grind out and take a couple steps closer to her. "You can't just walk in here acting like you've been her mother after the last couple years." Before I reach the steps, I turn to look at her over my shoulder and say, "Get the hell out of my house before I call the cops."

Arabella's cries are echoing down the hall and each sob cracks another piece of my heart. I wait until I hear the front door slamming before I push Arabella's door open and walk over to her bed, pulling her into my chest. "You don't have to stay up here, Bug. I told her to leave."

She wipes at her eyes and looks at me with a frown. "Why would she say that about Wrenly? She's a nice person."

"I'm not sure, Arabella, but don't worry about your mother." The last thing I'm going to do is talk bad about Erica to our daughter, that's never been something I do. My mind can't help but run back to Wrenly as I keep my arms wrapped around Arabella.

I know why Erica is threatened. She can tell I'm feeling something for Wrenly and she can't handle someone else having my attention. All she wants is someone to lean back on when things don't go her way and she stupidly thought I'd always be here for her.

That was a wrong move on her part. With each beat of my heart, I know I need to figure out a way to get Wrenly back. The issue with that though? When I tried calling her as soon as I saw she was gone, the number I had for her was disconnected. Which means there's no way for me to get ahold of her, and no way for me to know where she went.

She could've easily gone back to the ex she ran away from. I know he was bothering her since being here, it probably wouldn't have taken much for her to give in to his pull. The thought of her running right back to him, after getting close to us, has my blood boiling with jealousy.

And a bigger need to get her back to us.

Chapter 25

Wrenly

I t's been a week.

A week since I left Blake's and took residence in this bed and breakfast. I've spent every morning since sitting in the dining room, watching everyone come and go from the place. Meanwhile, I'm too chicken shit to walk out the door myself. I'm afraid I'll end up catching Blake walking around with Erica and that's not something I want to witness.

The situation I'm finding myself in, though, is that I don't want to leave Iris Springs. Not only because of the single dad and his daughter who wormed their way into my system, but because it's a great place. I've never felt more at peace anywhere else, and that's why I've yet to find a new job.

My two weeks are almost up and I'm trying to convince myself that I need to get out of town, find somewhere else to go, but my heart is begging me to stay. There's a small alcove situated in front of the window in the sitting room and I jump from the spot when an older couple comes into the room. They're smiling at each other with nothing but love in their eyes and it has my heart aching.

This could be me one day and the only person I could imagine looking at like that is the same man I ran away from last week. My ex has been trying to get a hold of me, so I did the logical thing and changed my number as soon as I left Blake's. Unfortunately, that means if Blake has tried contacting me in the last week, he would've failed at his attempts.

Don't be ridiculous, Wrenly, he doesn't need you to take up his time anymore. He'll have Erica to do that. The name alone has my vision turning red, but the color immediately fades away when the older woman who walked in taps on my shoulder with a small smile.

"Hello, dear, could I bother you for a moment?"

Even though I'm not feeling it, this is one of the reasons I want to stay here. It doesn't matter who it is, everyone in this town talks to you, wants to know how you're doing, and everything else that makes you tick. I give her a soft smile and nod. "Of course."

She glances at the spot I'm sitting in and asks, "Could I possibly sit here for a little while?" Her hand comes up, which has a crossword puzzle book tucked within her fist, and she shakes it. "The natural light is good for thinking."

I lift from my spot by the window, then wave my hand out over the now empty space. "It's all yours." Before I walk out of the room, I give who I'm assuming is her husband a small nod, then scurry up the steps away from everyone else.

As much as I love how involved this town is with each other, it's not something I'm particularly enjoying at the moment. I'd much rather stay in this room and not have to deal with a single human, but unfortunately, Belinda, the owner of this fine establishment, wouldn't let me do that.

Considering how small of a town this is it didn't take much for some residents to figure out what the hell is going on. I mean, there was an image with me, Blake, and Arabella from one of the rodeos plastered everywhere. Belinda is the only one who's managed to get me talking and I'm not too proud of it. Since then though, she's made it her mission to make sure I'm getting out of the tiny room that looks like someone vomited up flowers throughout.

I mean, seriously.

There's floral pattern wallpaper glued to each wall, the bed set has roses all over it, and even the dresser has porcelain flowers stacked on top of it. Just looking at it sends a shiver rolling through me. I'm sure the sunshine and fresh air would do me good right now, but the fear of what I'll see when I walk out the front door is too much for me right now.

Clearly, my favorite thing to do is run — first I end up in this town in the first place, then I end up practically becoming a hobbit at the bed and breakfast. Maybe I should stop running, but I'm not sure where I would go. There's one person I haven't talked to in a while who could probably give me some clarity.

Will she be willing to do that though?

I guess there's only one way to find out.

Since I changed my number, I have to text Celia and let her know it's me before I hit the call button under her name. It rings a few times before stopping, the sound of heaving breathing loud in my ear. "Cece?"

A loud crash has me jumping, then Celia's letting out a string of curses. "Shit," she mutters. "Sorry, Lee, I'm in the middle of a big piece that needs to be ready by next week."

The sound of the nickname she gave me burns through me and I try to keep the tears back. Celia is an upcoming artist who has the opportunity of a lifetime, as long as she can finish two new paintings to put into the art gallery event. She's been dreaming of a moment like this all her life and there's no one more deserving than her. I feel like I shouldn't be bothering her, which is the exact reason why I haven't gotten in touch until now.

I sigh into the phone. "It's okay, I didn't mean to interrupt. Anything ruined?"

She chuckles. "Only the hardwood floor under me, but it's no biggie." There's shuffling on the other end before she asks, "What's up?"

"What makes you think something's up?"

I can already see her rolling her eyes at me, one of her favorite things to do, and it brings a much-needed smile to my face. Maybe this is what I was missing, a feeling of normalcy. "Lee, you haven't called me in weeks." And now I feel like a shitty friend. "Which is fine," she states as if she was able to read my thoughts.

"Are you sure?"

"I've been swamped myself, so I'm not sure how much I would've been able to talk anyway. How's everything going?"

The last time I talked to her she was getting a rundown of everything going on with Blake and me, and now I'm wallowing alone in a room that's not close to him. I scoff and pick at the string hanging from my sweater. "Not great."

"Wanna talk about it?"

I run a hand through my hair, trying to think about what I want to tell her and what I'd like to keep inside for just a little while longer. "Well, I'm in a tough spot and thought you could give me your best friend advice."

She chuckles. "Well, that's what I'm here for. Let me hear it."

"I left a week ago and I've been staying at the bed and breakfast not far from his house. I'm not sure I want to leave and thought you could give me your feelings on the matter."

Celia sighs on the other end. "Well, Lee, judging by the way everything has been lately... I say stay there." Before I can question why she thinks that, she continues. "I've never heard you talk so vibrantly about someone before and I think you should explore that."

Just the idea of her believing in whatever Blake and I share has a sob escaping my throat that I was trying so desperately to hide.

"What's going on?" Celia asks, nothing but concern laced in her voice. She's truly the sister I never had growing up.

I shake my head. "It's complicated."

"So, uncomplicate it."

"It's not that simple, Cece. It involves Arabella's mother."

She hums in response to that, then clears her throat. "What happened?"

"He was kissing her last week, at the exact moment I was going to go up to him and admit all of my feelings." It was the most tortuous moment I've ever witnessed. Wanting more than anything to run up into his arms, but knowing that he had someone better in them already. That's why I needed to leave. I can't torture myself any longer.

"Listen, Lee, as much as you've been hurting, I still think you owe it to yourself and your heart to tell him what's going on. Tell him how you feel and find out if he feels the same way."

My breath hitches and I blink against the tears. "W-what if he doesn't feel the same way about me?"

"That's the thing about love, Lee, it hurts you deeply. The only thing you can do when that happens is heal from it, and I believe you're strong enough to do that." She sighs. "I need to get back to this painting, but I say go for it. All of it." We say our goodbyes before she's quickly hanging up to get back to her work.

I drop the phone onto the mattress beside me then fling back against the spring material. This is ridiculous — to be considering the vulnerability. What do I do if I look like a complete idiot telling him how I feel, especially after being gone without contacting him for a week? Nothing good could come of this, no matter what Celia says.

When Celia and I were little girls in middle school, the year she moved into my neighborhood, we immediately became friends. The moment she stood up for me, on her first day, to a boy in our class, I knew we'd be inseparable. And we were. It wasn't long after our first initial meeting that we made up nicknames for each other — I used the first two letters of her name, and she chose to use the last two of my name.

Cece and Lee. When everything was much easier than it is now.

I blow out a rough breath and curl into the heavy blanket spread out under me, then close my eyes slowly. I'm trying my hardest to believe this could turn out to be a good thing. Worst case is that he doesn't feel anything for me and it's all been one-sided. Best case?

He could feel what I feel and it would bring me nothing but happiness.

Is a possible broken heart worth the best man I've ever known?

Of course he is, but what about Erica?

Arabella is so young, I'm sure she'd love nothing more than to have her mother back in her life. What kind of person would I be if I jeopardized that for her? If I put my own feelings ahead of hers? Terrible, that's what. I could never risk the relationship Arabella could have with Erica, even if it means letting everything unfold from behind the scenes.

What if he's trying to find you right now?

I shake my head at the thought. This isn't some kind of fairytale where the prince magically shows up after searching for me for weeks or months. That's not how the real world works. He's probably relaxing in his house right this minute, Arabella curled up in his arms, while Erica makes them dinner.

A big happy family.

Maybe I should completely ignore the conversation with Celia and get the hell out of this town. Let Blake live his life the way he wants to — without me involved. When it comes time for the next rodeo, I'm sure he'll be able to find a new nanny to fill my shoes.

I nod. That's exactly what I'll do. It's what would be best for everyone.

So, why does the thought of it make my stomach roll over with sickness?

Chapter 26

Blake

I've been sitting here for a couple hours now nursing an untouched glass of bourbon. I haven't drank alcohol in years, ever since Arabella was just a little girl, and now I'm struggling not to take a sip of the dark liquid in front of me. It was a mistake to come here and hope that everything would be okay, that I would be able to get through it.

I glance around the small crowd gathered around the bar, looking for a flash of blonde hair that I know won't be there. I'm pathetic. It's been a week since she left and I'm still determined to figure out where she went and bring her back to Arabella and me.

My phone pings from my pocket with a text message from Erica, letting me know she's going to be picking Arabella up in the morning after a meeting. That's a new development this week — Erica is actually trying, which is more than I gave her credit for. I was convinced the only reason she was so involved was because of jealousy.

There's a live band standing at the front of the room that I turn to watch, seeing as there's nothing else to do in this place right now.

Sitting here reminds me of the night Wrenly walked in here and blew me away. Even then I couldn't seem to take my eyes off her. She was confident in a way that made her incredibly sexy and made me want to stick close to her.

If only I had known how much that night would change my life.

Squealing from behind me has me turning to look over my shoulder, eyeing the younger guy with his hands around a woman's waist, then I go to look back. Another squeal puts me on high alert and I eye the two of them curiously.

My eyes zero in on the hands he has on her waist, that he keeps trying to dip further down her body, but she's trying to wiggle away from him. It wasn't squeals of joy I was hearing, she's in need of some help. Luckily for her, I'm a man with enough stress humming throughout my body that it's in need of a release. What better way than to knock this guy out?

I quickly stand, leaving my bourbon on the bar top still untouched, and push through another couple who steps in front of me. That's the thing I hate most about drunks, they act a mess. Could never imagine what I looked like while I was drinking all the time — stumbling up and down stairs, mumbling to myself and making little to no sense. I know some who make the weirdest concoctions out of food.

When I reach the couple and lock eyes with the woman he's caging in, I bring a finger to my lips as a gesture of silence. She closes her eyes, acting like she's into the moment, then I grab the guy by the back of his shirt and throw him onto the floor. He scrambles to get up with a glare pointed in my direction, before he's standing tall with his hands out in fists in front of him.

"I think you should leave while you still can," he spits out.

While the woman tries to wrap her hand around my arm to stop me, I do the only thing I can think of right now and shake her off before heading toward the guy. I'm not in my right mind at the moment. If I were, I would've walked away from this, not garnered the attention I'm sure to receive... but I can't do that.

My hands are itching to connect with his face as I take the steps to close the distance between us. He smirks at me, then chuckles. "What's wrong? Couldn't manage to keep the nanny in your bed so now you're trying to find someone new?" How the hell does he know about her?

I mentally smack myself. Of course he knows, you can't put anything past anyone in this town, but his words make me tense. "Watch your mouth," I warn. It's the only one he'll get before my fist connects with his jaw.

He sneers at me, looking my body up and down. "I guess I can see why she would stop coming back to you, old man. She probably needs someone a little more capable... more her own age." The moment his eyes roll into the back of his head, I know I'm about to snap at his next words. "Maybe she'll let me take her for a spin, show her what a real man can do."

I barely blink as I connect a right hook to his jaw and he stumbles back a few steps with a smile. There's blood trickling from the corner of his mouth that he wipes away, then he's got his gaze narrowed on me. "You don't want to do this right now, man."

I should take the warning, but I'm not one for making the best decisions for myself right now.

Hence the reason I'm here in the first place, trying to hang around and see if Wrenly makes an appearance here. I'm not sure what it is, but there's this feeling deep in my gut that she's still in town, and I'm determined to find her before she skips it. What could she possibly still be doing here though? She had every opportunity to head somewhere new, yet she chose to stay here — that is, as long as my gut is right.

This could all be wishful thinking and she really did skip town as soon as she left. I'd like to think that the last few months have meant more to her than that though and she'd be more likely to stick around. When I went to Belinda's place, she wouldn't tell me anyone by the name of Wrenly was staying at her bed and breakfast, but she also gave me a wicked grin.

I'm so lost in my head about Wrenly that I don't see the guy come at me until it's too late. There's a loud snap as my left side connects with the floor and it takes everything in me not to scream out in pain. When the guy stands, he towers above me with a smile before walking away as if he didn't just break something on my body. It's got to be my arm.

When I look down, there is already a large bruise forming over my arm and it's hanging loosely over my stomach. Definitely broken. The girl from before walks over to me and gives me a small smile in thanks, then gets an ambulance on the line. I'm being loaded into the back of one with a bunch of lights flashing around me, mostly townspeople wanting to get their fifteen minutes of fame by getting a picture of me.

There's a nursing staff waiting just inside the emergency room doors when we pull in front of them and they hurry out to help them get me inside unnoticed. I'm sure the last thing they need is a mob outside the place trying to get a peek at me.

I'm sure it's the shock, but the only thing I feel is a dull ache in my arm. If Wrenly hadn't been a permanent fixture in my head, this never would've happened.

I could continue blaming her, but that wouldn't be entirely fair. Things could've gone differently and they didn't, because I couldn't seem to keep up with the professional line I put between the two of us before she started. One of the nurses gives me a nervous smile as she leads the paramedics down a long hallway and into the last room on the right.

She helps them get me into the hospital bed, which looks a lot comfier than the chair, and takes a look at my arm. The moment her fingers come up to it, I hiss at the pain from her touch. "Sorry. The doctor will be in shortly. You'll have to be put in a cast I'm sure, but he will let you know more when he comes in."

I nod and clear my throat. "Could you block off this hallway from any other patients?"

"Uh, I'm not sure we are able to do that, sir."

"Blake is fine, sir makes me feel old." And after that sideways comment that guy made, I'd rather not think about me being old right now. Is that why Wrenly left so quickly? She realized she liked me, had feelings for me, but thought I was too old? I shake my head and groan into the empty room.

Thirty minutes later there's a soft knock at the door and it's being pushed open. I sit up straighter in the hospital bed, but my energy turns cold when Erica walks through the room. She situates a large bag on the floor beside my bed and leans down to give me a soft kiss on the forehead. I flinch away from her touch, but it seems as if she isn't aware of the movement and smiles at me.

"Gosh, I'm so glad you're okay. What happened?"

I blink a couple times and shake my head. "What are you doing here?"

She chuckles. "Well, they called me."

That can't be right. When I was filling out paperwork before the rodeo started, I put Wrenly on the papers as my emergency contact and I still haven't taken her off. If they called anyone, it wasn't Erica. I glare at her. "Well, you aren't needed here."

'That's not what the doctor said." Then she takes a seat like I never uttered a single word to her. Why the hell won't she listen to me?

I growl low in my throat. "Erica, leave."

"You need to calm down, honey." She tries running her hands through my hair but I dart away from her touch and the surprise is clear on her face.

"I already told you, Erica. You and I are done, which I meant. There's someone else and I'd like to see where it will go, but I can't do that with you always hanging around."

Erica chuckles softly and nods. "I guess I should've taken the hint when you said something the first time." She stands slowly from the chair beside the bed whil smiling at me and pats my good arm. "This was merely me making sure you were okay, but I'll go ahead and leave."

"Are you going to continue having a relationship with Arabella?" I'd hate for Erica to walk out of her life again simply because I didn't want a romantic relationship with her.

"You know, I think I am," she says with a smile. "I've been gone for far too long and it's about time I stepped up." Her gaze darts to the door and she smiles. "I'm happy for you even if I haven't shown it."

I nod in acknowledgment, then watch as she steps quietly outside the room and the door shuts behind her with a soft click. How the hell am I supposed to find Wrenly when I'm stuck in this hospital room until further notice?

I shouldn't be here too much longer, though — I'll find her when I'm out.

Unless you don't need to.

A smile takes over my face at the thought of Wrenly getting a call about me in the hospital and running back to me. Maybe I'll be seeing her soon after all. My body heats as another knock sounds on the door and Wrenly pokes her head inside quickly, scanning the rest of the room. When she's satisfied, her steps are sure and quick as she heads over to the bed.

Those chocolate-colored eyes will never cease to amaze me.

Chapter 27

Wrenly

I'm sitting in the alcove at the bed and breakfast with a book open on my lap when Belinda walks quickly into the room with me. She stands there in awkward silence for a few seconds, then she clears her throat. "I wasn't sure if you'd like to know, but Blake was taken to the emergency room tonight."

The moment she finishes speaking, I'm jumping from the spot and hurrying through the sitting room.

"When did he get taken there?" I ask, glancing over my shoulder to look at her.

She shrugs. "I'm not sure, hon, but maybe you could go see him?" Judging by the small smile she's giving me, I'd say she's enjoying trying to get us back into each other's lives.

"What hospital is he at?"

"Iris Springs General."

I take a deep breath and rush into the room I'm staying in, then throw a pair of pajamas on. There's no time to see how I look, not when Blake is sitting in a hospital room right now.

Belinda smirks as she gazes at my outfit, but I ignore it and hurry past her to head downstairs. "Do you know what happened?"

"Something about a bar fight, that's all I heard."

Shit. What the hell was he doing getting into a bar fight? I shake my head and grab my keys from the hook hanging by the front door. Belinda follows behind me until I get to the driver's side of the car and I give her a grateful smile. "Thank you for letting me know." Then I'm getting into the car and rushing toward the hospital.

What about Arabella?

I could head straight to the hospital, but what if Arabella is worried about where her dad is? Instead of going in the direction of the hospital, I make a right turn and head in the direction of Blake's ranch. The only light on is in the living room when I pull up and I jump when the front porch light turns on as I step out of the car.

The front door opens and Blake's mother pokes her head out, squinting under the light to see who's here. She smiles when I walk up the steps and ushers me inside. "Wrenly, dear, what are you doing here so late?"

I blink in confusion. "Uh, have you not heard anything?"

His mother frowns at me. "I'm not sure what you mean. Is everything okay?"

"Well, Belinda just told me that Blake is in the hospital."

She gasps and brings a hand to her mouth, eyes glistening. "I-is he alright?"

I shrug. "I'm not sure. I was on my way there, but didn't know if Arabella would be worried about him so figured I'd stop here first."

Her smile isn't bright, but it's enough to give me the reassurance I need that this was the right move to make. It falls quickly. "Erica rushed out of here a little bit ago, wouldn't tell me where she was going."

Of course she wouldn't because she wants all of Blake's attention on her.

I sigh. "Maybe he doesn't need me to stop by, since Erica is already there with him."

His mother shakes her head and gives me a warm smile. Blake has the exact same smile and I find myself getting teary-eyed at the realization. She places her hand on my shoulder and says, "I'd really love it if you would stop by, so I can at least know what's going on."

How could I possibly deny her that?

She's been sitting here, waiting for him to get home, and I show up to tell her he's in the hospital? I'm sure she's terrified. I'll go there, try to get into his room, and hopefully get enough out of him to relay back to his mother. She deserves at least that much, and it only irritates me that Erica wouldn't let her know what's going on.

I sigh and give her a small nod. "Sure, I can do that." Before I leave, I plug my new number into her phone, that way if I try calling her she won't be confused by a random number. "As soon as I know anything, I'll call you. But, don't worry, if it was that bad I'm sure someone would've come by already or called your phone."

It's the only reassurance I can try to give her.

It doesn't take me long to pull into the parking lot of the hospital and rush through the large sliding doors. There's a young girl sitting

189

behind a thick slab of glass and she gives me a barely-there smile. "Hi, what do you need to be seen for?"

I shake my head and say, "I'm not here to be seen. My name is Wrenly and I'm here for Blake, he came in a little bit ago."

The girl nods and frowns at me. "I'm sorry, ma'am, but visiting hours are over right now."

"Are you able to give me any information at all? I'm the nanny for his daughter and would like to be able to tell her something." Maybe the whole nanny thing will let me get this information easily.

She sighs. "I can't disclose medical information without the patient's consent. Would you give me a moment?" Before I can respond, she's lifting from a chair and walking through a door in the back, then coming out a few minutes later. "It looks like the hospital tried calling you when he got in, but the number was disconnected."

I cock my head to the side. "Why would they try calling me?"

"It looks like you're his emergency contact." She scrolls through the computer, then prints something out and hands it to me through the opening at the bottom of the glass. "This is a visitor pass. Since you're his emergency contact, you're allowed to go up there with him."

My heart beats rapidly, knowing I'm about to walk in there and Erica will be at his side worrying over him. I should be the one sitting next to him. It should've been me that was sitting here as soon as he came in.

"Thank you," I say softly.

The woman leads me through the halls until we get to one that's completely deserted, except for the one that's at the end on the right. She's about to knock, but when I hear Blake and Erica talking, I

190

place my hand on her shoulder to stop her. "I'll go in shortly, you don't have to bother him right now."

She nods, unsure of my request, but heads back out to the waiting room where I entered. I lean against the wall right next to the door and angle my head a little closer, hoping I can get bits and pieces of their conversation. There are muffled voices inside, but they seem to get slightly louder.

My heart jumps at Blake's voice and the words coming out of his mouth. There's someone else? He's not happy she's in the room with him right now, which isn't something I was prepared for, but I can't help the way my heart slows down in my chest. Could he be talking about me?

I push away from the wall when I hear Erica say she's going to head out and that she's happy for him. She didn't notice me behind the door and I watch as she slowly makes her way out of the room and goes in the same direction as the receptionist. Maybe it's better if I give it a few minutes, let him get his feelings under control, then I'll walk into the room.

Before I knock on the door, I take a deep breath and situate myself in front of the door. There's a rectangular window that I can peek through, or he could see me if he looked, so I make sure to steer clear of it as I lift my fist to the thick wood.

The sound echoes through the empty hallway and I slowly ease the door open, then step through with my breath caught in my throat. Even though I told Blake's mom that I'm sure he's fine, I don't know that for sure, and I'm worried about what I'll see when I get a look at him.

My shoulders sag in relief when I catch sight of him in the hospital bed. There's a small bruise on his jaw, but otherwise the only thing I can see is the cast on his arm. Blake's silent as he watches me move closer to him and sit down in the chair next to his bed.

It's not awkward though. More like we are communicating with our ragged breaths. He leans forward and places his hand on my knee, his heated gaze shining on me before giving me a small smile. "Wrenly, it's fancy seeing you here."

I glare at him. "What the hell were you thinking getting into a bar fight?"

He groans and throws his head back against the fluffed pillows behind him. "It was a reaction."

"That's all you got?"

Blake shakes his head and levels me with a frown. "No. He was talking about you in a way I didn't appreciate, so I lashed out." He shrugs and pulls his hand away from mine. "I'm not sorry for it, he's lucky he knocked me on the ground when he caught me off guard, or else he'd be the one sitting here."

He fought for me?

I eye him curiously. "What did he say?"

His gaze softens and he shakes his head. "Please don't make me repeat it." His body is tense as he spaces out for a second, probably thinking about the events of the night, and I choose to let it go. If he wants to tell me later on, he will, but I won't force him to do so. "What are you doing here?"

"Belinda told me you were here, then your mother convinced me to come."

He scrunches his eyebrows together in confusion. "My mom?"

I nod and give him a nervous smile. "I went to check on Arabella, in case she was worried about you. Turns out your mom didn't even know you got sent here and Erica left without saying anything to her."

His jaw clenches and he growls. "Of course not." Then he brings his hand back to me and threads his fingers through mine. "Thank you for stopping by the house, it means a lot to me."

"Don't mention it."

He's looking at me as if he wants to say something, but I'm not sure I'm ready to hear it right now. Either he's going to tell me our feelings are mutual, or he's going to reject me right here and now. I'm not sure my heart is ready for it to be the latter. We stare at each other for a few minutes and Celia's voice runs through my mind.

Maybe she's right. Sometimes, it hurts, but what if we live the rest of our lives wondering *what if?* That's not something I'm willing to do. Not if it means I can stay by his side.

I open my mouth, ready to tell him how I feel, but he brings a finger to my lips and silences me. Why isn't he letting me talk? There's a sinking feeling in my belly, but I don't open my mouth to say anything. If he doesn't want me talking right this second, then that's what I'll do. I'll sit here silently and wait for him to say whatever he needs to.

I'm just hoping what he needs to say is along the same lines as what I was going to say. That I haven't been able to stop thinking about him since I left last week, no matter how I tried. I've laid in bed at night, wondering what Arabella is up to or if either of them were upset about me being gone.

Chapter 28

Blake

She's staring at me patiently, waiting for me to get the words out, but my mouth is dry and I can't seem to bring myself to say anything. I look to my left, where a tray is sitting, and grab the small cup of water that's sitting there. Once the cold liquid slides down my throat, I take a deep breath and give her hand a squeeze.

Her breaths are ragged as she watches me and I study her for a moment. I can't help but smirk at the pajamas covering her body — cats cover each leg of the pants she's wearing, and there's a single cat head in the middle of her shirt. I look back up into her eyes and give her a wink. "Nice PJ's."

Wrenly blinks, then looks down at her clothes as if she didn't realize what she put on, then her cheeks grow red. "Oh, God," she mutters while covering her face with her hands.

I reach up and pull them away with a smile. "No need to be embarrassed, I was being serious." It's nice to see her looking out of character. She doesn't have a single drop of makeup on, which is one of my favorite looks on her. Without makeup it seems as though her brown eyes shine brighter.

I brush my knuckles over her skin, enjoying the way her breath hitches at my touch and how she leans into it. "Blake," she whispers.

"Wrenly, there's something I need to say."

She nods, her body tensing at the statement, and I realize she probably thinks the worst is going to come out of my mouth. I bring my fingers to the tip of her chin and lift her face level to mine. "I've made a huge mistake."

"I figured you were going to say that," she says with a chuckle and shakes her head.

"I made a huge mistake by letting you walk away so easily," I say, keeping my gaze locked on hers and watching as her eyes dart back and forth. "This entire time I should've been embracing the feelings I have for you, rather than pushing them away."

"Feelings?"

I nod and smile at her. "I've never felt this way about anyone before, not even Erica, and I was scared of what those feelings meant. Scared of what you could do to me with those feelings."

She frowns. "What does that mean?"

"Erica left as soon as someone better came along, and I didn't want the same thing to happen with you. So I kept my heart chained up, built steel walls around it, that way I wouldn't be able to get hurt in the end." I shake my head and let out a rough breath. "It ended up happening anyway."

"I didn't want to hurt you."

"*You* didn't hurt me. I hurt myself when I didn't let you know how I felt." I sigh and shake my head. "But I can't do that anymore. I've never felt freer than I have with you."

Wrenly smiles and a tear falls down her cheek that I catch with the tip of my thumb. I'm caught by surprise when her arms wrap around me a second later, and I breathe in her scent. Fruit. I've never loved the smell of fruit so much as I do right now.

When she pulls away from me, she dabs at her eyes and shakes her head. "God, I'm pathetic."

I frown at her. "Don't talk about yourself like that, you're anything but. You're beautiful, real, and amazing." My mind goes back to all the ways she treated Arabella as her own and I smile at her. "I've never watched anyone interact with Arabella in the way you have, and that's when I knew this was going to be harder to ignore than I hoped." I shake my head. "I'm not ignoring it anymore though, Wrenly."

"I don't want you to ignore it." She presses her forehead against mine, lips centimeters away from my own, and I'm about to connect them when there's a light tap on the door. Wrenly quickly pushes away from me, casually leaning back against the chair next to me, and watches as the doctor walks through the room.

The doctor gives me a smile and nods at Wrenly. "Blake, I think it's about time we get you home. You've only got a broken arm, nothing else seems to be wrong, so you're free to go as long as you feel comfortable."

"Yes, please," I say, moving my hand next to me until my skin connects with Wrenly's. She gives my hand a gentle squeeze, while I answer questions for the doctor, then wait for him to come back with the discharge papers.

When we get out into the parking lot, Wrenly helps me inside her car, then walks around to the driver's side. She called my mom a few minutes ago to let her know that I was on my way back home, and she was thankful that Wrenly still came by the hospital for her.

I want to ask her why she was thinking about not coming, but I don't want to ruin the charge in the air that's present. She eases the car out onto the main road, which is pitch black, then makes a left onto the back road leading to my house. When we pull in front of my house my mom is already standing outside on the front porch and walks down the steps eagerly to wrap me in her arms.

"I was worried as soon as Wrenly told me what was going on. I'm glad it wasn't anything too serious."

When I look over, I expect to see Wrenly standing outside the car, but she's nowhere in sight. I lean down and find her still sitting in the driver's seat of her car which is still vibrating with power. She jumps when I knock on the window, then rolls it down.

"What are you doing?" I ask.

She smiles. "Uh, going back to Belinda's?"

I'm still trying to understand why Belinda wouldn't tell me that Wrenly was staying at the bed and breakfast, but I'm not sure that matters so much right now. Not when Wrenly knows how I feel and it seems as though she feels the same way.

My mother chuckles next to me and gives me another small squeeze before heading down the driveway toward her own car. I watch as she backs out, leaving me standing alone in the night air with Wrenly sitting in the car.

"Come inside, Wrenly." There's no way I'm letting her leave right now. Not after everything that has been said tonight. I want to fall asleep with her next to me, wake up to see how Arabella reacts to Wrenly being back here.

"Are you sure?" Maybe she's worried about what Arabella might think, but I'm not as worried as she might be. I think Arabella would be happy about the turn of events, and even more happy to have Wrenly back in our lives.

"Absolutely," I say with a smile.

My hands are itching to run over her smooth skin and I hope she's ready for it. She slowly gets out of the car and follows me up the steps in silence.

Once I get everything locked up and all the lights shut out, I head upstairs and peek in at Arabella sleeping peacefully across her bed. I'm not sure where that girl gets her sleeping habits from — one minute she will be sleeping normally, then the next her head will be hanging off the bed without a care in the world.

Even Erica didn't sleep like that.

I thread my fingers through Wrenly's and pull her into my room, then over to the bed as I shut the door behind us. Her chest is rising and falling with her breaths, forcing me to trace my finger over the skin showing along her neck. Her body trembles, but she doesn't make a move to pull away from me, which only gives me the push I need to keep going.

There may be a cast on my arm, but that doesn't mean I can't please her tonight. I wouldn't want to do anything more than listen to her cry out my name with my tongue on her. When I push her back into the bed, she gasps and falls down. I hover above her and bring my lips to hers in an all-consuming kiss.

She deepens it immediately, bringing her hands to my head and pushing me further into her, while wrapping her legs around my waist. The front of my pants bulges, alerting her of what she does to me, and I rock my hips into her center. She clenches her legs tighter around me, basking in the feel of me against her even though she's covered by clothes.

Not for much longer though.

I run my hand down the length of her body until I reach the waist-band of her pants and push them slowly down her legs. Once off, I throw them onto the floor and go for the hem of her shirt. I groan at the sight of her bare chest, nipples poking out in invitation, and bring my mouth around one. She arches her back into me, begging me for more with her movements, and I use a free hand to pinch her other nipple.

She gasps at the action and rocks her hips into me, wishing for a release that only I can give. I lift my mouth away from her breasts, then glide my tongue down the length of her stomach until I reach the black lace panties she's wearing.

With my teeth hooked into the fabric, I ease my body down hers and pull the panties along with me, letting them drop to the floor after I get them past her ankles.

There's a small palm tree tattooed along the length of her foot and I trail my tongue over it, eliciting a gasp from Wrenly above me. I smirk against her skin, then travel back up until my tongue is flattening against her slick center. I'm doing my best not to push onto my casted arm, so I use my other one to grip her hip as I dive deeper into her.

It's heaven.

Pure heaven.

I moan against her soft, silky skin at the same time she moans into the dark room. It's the sweetest sound I've ever heard. I'm not sure why it took me so long to admit the way I feel about her, but I'll spend the rest of my life proving it all. Making sure she believes I want her.

This is how I start.

———

Wrenly is breathing evenly against me as I look up at the ceiling. I'm too wired to fall asleep right now, but refuse to get up when I finally have her in my arms. In my bed. I rub my fingers along the small of her back and smile into the dark room, happier now that she's here.

I'll wake up to her in the morning and I've never been happier about that. Once Erica left, I thought this feeling was going to be gone forever, but it's only getting started. The feelings I had for Erica all those years ago are nothing compared to the ones running through me for Wrenly.

I wrap my arm tighter around Wrenly when she snuggles closer to me in her sleep, then press a tender kiss to the top of her head. This is the life Arabella and I deserve to have. Wrenly's done nothing but love on my daughter and that's the best thing I could've ever asked for.

Now it's almost time to break the news to Arabella in the morning and I'm almost certain she will be ecstatic about it.

Chapter 29

Wrenly

I didn't think it'd feel so amazing to wake up covered in nothing but warmth from Blake's body against mine. His loud snores have my shoulders shaking with laughter as I lift up and gently move out from in front of him, careful not to hurt his broken arm in the process. When I finish using the bathroom, I smile at Blake's sleeping form on the bed, then snap my gaze to the door when I hear the soft footsteps walking down the hall.

Shit. Arabella.

My hands shake at the thought of telling her about the two of us, but I also know it's not something that we can keep from her. I walk quietly back over to the bed and sit at the edge of it, my gaze trained out the window where the sun only gets brighter and brighter as it lifts on the horizon.

I jump at Blake's hand coming down on my leg, then turn to find his eyes locked on me. "Good morning," he whispers to me with a smile, then he leans up and presses a quick kiss to my lips before getting out of bed himself.

The shower turns on, but I don't make a move to join him. If he wants me in there with him, he'll tell me that, and maybe last night wasn't what I thought it was. That thought alone has my body dripping with sweat. What if he just wanted another amazing night with me before he sends me away from here?

I've yet to tell him what happened with my ex, but maybe it's time I do that. It would give him an understanding of why my first instinct was to run away from the situation with Erica. I take a deep breath and head into the bathroom, my eyes traveling down the length of his naked frame, then coming back up to meet his heated gaze.

I clear my throat, not wanting to get into something without telling him what I need to. "I, uh, never told you anything about that ex of mine." His gaze is boring into mine, letting me know he's hanging on to every word I'm saying and I lean against the bathroom sink. "It was our anniversary the night I ran away."

It sucks that I can remember the moment so vividly still.

"I was supposed to work and I did, but they let me go home early since it was a slow day. As a gift, I stopped at one of our usual spots to grab some dinner, then bought him this baseball cap that he'd been raving about." I chuckle at the memory. "Thinking back, I ignored all the red flags. Anyway, when I got through our front door there was this feeling in my gut I couldn't ignore."

Blake turns the water off and steps out, instantly wrapping the towel around himself so he doesn't distract me from the story. This man could distract me even if he had a paper bag over his head.

But, that's not what I'm talking about right now.

I take a deep breath and smile at Blake. "It was silent for a few minutes, until a thump came from upstairs in our room. Like an idiot, I went to inspect the noise." Just thinking about the image I saw has red clouding my vision. "When I pushed the door to our room open, there he was, kneeling on the bed in front of some naked woman, and that's when I ran out. I grabbed anything I could get my hands on after his side piece walked out, then I got in my car and never looked back."

Blake nods, still silent as if he's waiting for me to say more.

"That's why I ran after seeing you with Erica that night."

"Wrenly, I need you to know. That moment between me and Erica? It was all her. The only person I wanted to kiss that night was you. But then everything got out of control and I never got the chance to tell you that."

Blake closes the distance between us and I steal a glance down at the front of the towel, then look back up at him. There's a smirk on his face as he brings his good arm around my waist, pulling me against him and placing his lips a breath away from my own.

Then I remember Arabella is already awake and I push away from him with a shaky breath. "You have a little girl downstairs who's probably starving right now. Get dressed and we'll head downstairs together."

He nods, then heads out of the bathroom with me trailing right behind him. It's a very good position for me to look at his ass, which he catches immediately and winks at me.

I clear my throat and look around the room nervously. "Do you think she'll be okay with it?"

Blake sighs as he searches the room for clothes and gives me a reassuring smile. "I think that she will be more happy to see you than she's ever been about seeing me, so I think you should be grateful that she loves you so much."

Knowing that I may have hurt Arabella with how abruptly I left has a pit forming in the center of my stomach. "I'm sorry," I say softly.

He walks over to me and cradles my cheek with his hand. "For what, baby?"

I try to blink the years away, but they only fall rapidly down my face instead and I wipe them away. "For, uh, for hurting her. For not saying goodbye before I left. I thought I was doing the right thing."

Blake shakes his head and smiles. "You don't have to be sorry. You're here now, and that's all Arabella will worry about. Let's go enjoy some breakfast, then tell her about us and we will figure the rest out as time goes on." He threads his fingers between mine, then leads me out of the room. With each step we take downstairs, my heart beats a little harder in my chest.

Arabella's sitting in the kitchen with her back to us, scooping up spoonfuls of cereal and shoving them into her mouth. Seeing her dark curls brings an immediate smile to my face and I almost rush up to wrap my arms around her. Blake walks ahead of me to enter the kitchen and clears his throat, gaining Arabella's attention.

He gives me a small nod, letting me know to stop where I'm at, and I obey the command. Blake smiles at his daughter and says, "There's someone here for you."

Arabella's body tenses and she spins around, but her shoulders relax instantly at the sight of me and she rushes forward. The moment her arms wrap around my waist, the nerves that were taking over quickly dissipate as I squeeze her back. She pulls away with a big smile, but then it falls. "Why did you leave without saying goodbye?"

I sigh. "Hopefully one day I'll be able to tell you why, but for today just know that I'm sorry I left the way I did. At the time, I thought it was the right decision."

Arabella arches a brow. "And now?"

I smile at her. "Now? I think I'm right where I should've been all along."

"So, you're staying?" she asks, then turns her gaze over to her dad who gives her a small smile in response.

"Yeah, sweetie, I think I am. As long as that's okay with you, of course."

She screeches in delight and pulls me into her once again. "Are you kidding?" Then she pulls me into the living room to tell me all about her days with her mother, who doesn't seem to be all that bad now that she's done bothering Blake. Arabella's gaze darts between me and her father, then she smiles. I'm relieved Blake wasn't wrong about things. This went a lot better than I had convinced myself it would go. I thought that Arabella would hate me after the way I left her and Blake, but she's just as forgiving as her father even though I don't deserve it.

Things didn't have to be this complicated if I had just heard Blake out like he wanted in the beginning.

God, do these thoughts ever stop? I shake my head and walk around the space, my skin heating when Blake's body steps close to mine. His lips brush against the sensitive skin along my ear and he says, "Horse riding today?"

It seems like the perfect way to commemorate me being back on the ranch, back in these two amazing people's lives after being gone for seven days. Each of them were torturous without them and I never want to be apart that long again.

I nod and let him lead Arabella and me out to the horses.

While Blake and Arabella race in front of me on their horses, laughing at each other along the way, I can't help the bright smile that takes over my face. There's nothing quite like feeling whole with two people and getting that sense of belonging. My heart beats wildly in my chest at the thought of loving the man in front of me, but it's not out of fear. It's out of excitement.

This is bound to be an adventure of a lifetime, but what more could I ask for? Who knew that when I ran away, I'd find people to run towards and live my life with. I'm shaken from my thoughts when my phone rings in my pocket and I pull it out, smiling at Celia's name on the screen.

"Cece, hey," I say with a smile.

"Well?" she asks.

I sigh contently into the phone, my gaze still trained on my two favorite people in front of me, and say, "Let's just say, I think I'm home."

She squeals on the other end of the phone, causing me to move the phone away from my ear a little bit before she blows my ear drum out. "That's amazing, I'm so happy for you!"

"Thanks, Cece, I never would've made the step if I hadn't called you."

"Awe, I love you, Lee. I guess this means I need to come visit you out there?"

I smile at the thought. "I think that would be great. You'll love Blake's place and you'd probably hit it off with Arabella."

Cece chuckles, then someone says something to her in the background that has her groaning loudly. "I've gotta go, but I look forward to meeting Blake." She hangs up quickly and I sigh into the cool afternoon air.

Blake and Arabella finally come to a stop, then make their way back to me. I still haven't quite got the hang of horse riding, so I'm the slowest of the three of us, which Blake seems to find hilarious. I stick my tongue out at him, then spin the horse back in the direction of the barn area, and head toward it with my own smile on my face.

Blake tells Arabella to go get washed up inside while he follows me to the barn eagerly. As soon as I jump off the horse, he's coming up beside me and pushing me against the wall as his lips crash down onto mine.

I'll never get over the electric feeling his lips bring to me.

Epilogue

Blake

Being back on the road for the rodeo has been a little harder on me this year, especially since it's my last year and Wrenly has chosen to stay back with Arabella. Arabella has decided that she wants to be able to spend time with her friends, and she can't seem to do that if she's out traveling with me during the rodeo season. As much as I know Wrenly loves watching me in action, she loves making Arabella happy more.

Which only makes me love her more.

Erica gave it a chance for the first few weeks after the bar fight I got into, but it's been nothing but silence from her since then. I'm not sure why it's so hard for her to be a mother, but I'm grateful that Arabella now has someone else to fill that spot for her. I've never seen my daughter so happy.

I groan from the pain in my muscles as I jump down from the truck and squeeze my eyes shut for a moment to let it sink in. The lights are all out as I walk up the porch and I smile knowing I'm going to slip into bed with Wrenly in my arms, just as I have every night this entire time.

I'm not sure the idea of her being here will ever feel real to me, not when my heart has never felt more complete before in my life. It's like I'm living my best dream and I'm bound to wake up at some point, yet I never do. Nothing beats it. The lock clicks as I unlock the door and push it open softly, praying that I don't wake Wrenly in the process.

I lock the door behind me, then turn around and my eyes widen at the sight in front of me. There's what seems like a million candles lining the entryway, leading around the corner into the kitchen, where Wrenly stands behind the island with a big smile. She's got her hair pinned up on top of her head, which only tells me that she's more than ready for me to let it down later, and a black dress that looks like a second skin.

I eye her appreciatively, a smile pushing up on my lips. "What's all this?"

She shrugs and winks at me. "Guess you have to come in here and find out for yourself."

As I edge further into the room, there are two plates piled with food sitting on the table and more candles lit up around it. No wonder it was dark in here when I pulled up. I walk up to her and hold her in my arms and my body immediately reacts to the feeling of her breasts rubbing against me.

She pushes me away with a smile and presses her lips to mine in a soft kiss. I walk over to one of the empty chairs, pulling it out for her before making my way around the table to sit in the other one. Her eyes are looking at me curiously, as if trying to decide if she should tell me what's going on, then she darts her stare down to her plate.

Something is making her nervous, but what could it be?

When I push my last bite into my mouth, Wrenly lifts from the table and carries our dirty dishes over to the sink. She leaves them in there for tomorrow and reaches into one of the cabinets above the counter. I'm watching her curiously as she brings over a perfectly wrapped gift, her fingers toying with the ribbon hanging from it.

What could she have gotten me?

I'm pretty sure it's not our anniversary, and her birthday was last month. My birthday isn't for another three months. Is this something random that made her think of me and she isn't sure I'd appreciate it?

When she stops in front of me, her gaze locks onto the gift for a few seconds longer than normal, then she shakes her head as if in too much thought and hands it over to me. She smiles when I don't make a move to rip the paper open. "Well, go ahead, open the damn thing."

The slower I go about unwrapping it, the more nervous Wrenly seems to get, and that has me getting concerned. I glance around the house and ask, "Where's Arabella?"

"She's with your mother for the night, thought we could use some alone time." There's something more, but maybe that's what this gift is about.

As soon as I have the box open in front of me, a bright smile takes over my face and tears threaten to escape my eyes. I look up at her, blinking rapidly at the stinging sensation behind my eyes, and shake the box. "Are you sure?"

Wrenly nods frantically, her own eyes watering up, and I immediately bring her onto my lap. My lips slam into hers and I toss the box onto the table, not able to keep myself away from her right now. Her body is about to change in the most glorious way and I get to be the one to experience that with her. Arabella will be so happy about being a big sister, and I can't wait to tell her.

"I'm guessing you're happy?" Wrenly asks with a chuckle.

I smile at her and pull her closer to me. "Never been so happy in my entire life, this is the best gift I could've gotten. I love you, Wrenly."

Her cheeks turn bright pink and she smiles. "I love you more, Blake."

Then she's fusing our lips back together and straddling my lap as if she can't get enough of me. She rocks against me, giving herself the friction she needs, and I meet her rhythm with my own. Her deep breathing against my neck has my dick getting harder in my pants and I push them down my legs quickly.

Best night ever.

———

Wrenly

The sharp kick in my side has me grunting loudly next to Blake and he immediately turns his attention over to me. I roll my eyes and glare at him. "I'm fine, your son just thinks my ribs are a punching bag."

Melanie, Blake's mother, chuckles ahead of us and looks at Blake with a smile. "If women weren't made to handle it, we wouldn't. She's fine, son, trust me."

Blake nods, but I know he's been more on edge lately since the due date is approaching fast. We've got about two weeks left and nothing has been set up in the nursery, which Blake keeps promising he will do. Leave it to men to never get their shit done, which is why I enlisted Melanie's help with everything.

I refuse to push this baby out of me without everything being ready for him, and I'm feeling confident that I'll be going into labor soon. If I don't though, I'm being induced a week before our son's due date and I want it all set up now. The sooner the better.

Arabella skips over to us with a smile and throws a couple things for the baby into the cart as we walk around Target, eyeing every single thing that we see. Together we gush over all the different baby items, which Blake happily throws into the cart as he follows behind us.

If there's one thing about my husband I wish would come to an end, it's his need to give me everything I want. I've got everything I could ever want just with him and Arabella beside me, and now our newest addition, and nothing could ever beat their presence in my life.

"Sweetie," I say to Blake with a soft smile. "You don't have to get everything Arabella and I look at."

He smiles and gives me a quick kiss. "Anything my girl's want, they get." Then he throws something else into the cart without a glance at the price tag. It's a one hundred and fifty-dollar diaper bag, something we already have at home. Multiple, now that I think about it, because this is something Blake can't stop doing.

"Alright, well, I think it's time to head back and get things put together," Blake says. "Let's go, Arabella."

"Can I help you guys, Mom?"

Judging by the wetness of her eyes, Arabella calling her that still affects her more than she lets out. She plasters a smile on her face and nods, never able to tell her no when she brings the word mom into play. I shake my head, but smile because it's all I ever wanted for Arabella. To have someone that would spoil her just as much as I do, if not more.

———

It's close to two in the morning when the first wave of pain comes through and I hiss from it. I try to go as quietly as possible into the bathroom, figuring a bath might help me out, but as I'm about to get into the bathtub another wave of pain almost sends me to the ground.

"Blake!" I say through the contraction. These are real, I'm sure of it, and now I'm completely naked. "Blake, wake up!"

"Baby," Blake mumbles from the bedroom. "Wrenly, where are you?"

Another contraction makes me groan and he hurries into the bathroom with his eyes wide in panic. "It's time," I grind out with my hand pressed against my hard belly.

He rushes through the room for clothes and helps me put them on, then gets his phone to call his mom over. Before she's even pulling into the driveway, Blake has me in the car, with both mine and the baby's hospital bags at my feet, then he's peeling out of the lot without a word to his mom. While we fly through the back roads, I keep my eyes squeezed shut with each contraction that wracks through my body.

Why the hell did I sign up for this?

———

The piercing cry that fills the labor and delivery room answers my question from hours ago. As the doctor places the baby on my chest, putting my son's skin against mine, a tear falls down my face. This is why I signed up for this, because bringing a life into this world is the most amazing feeling. I've never felt as powerful as I did today.

Blake's hand comes up and runs over our son's head, a smile on his face even though there are tears falling from his eyes. He wipes at them, then gives me a beaming smile. "You were amazing, baby."

The praise coming from him only makes me feel even more powerful, like I can do anything. This life has been more than I ever thought it would be and I owe it all to the man standing next to me, with nothing but love in his eyes as he looks between me and our baby.

"What's his name?" the nurse who helped with the delivery asks.

I look over at Blake for the answer — our decision was that he would pick the name if it were a boy and I'd pick the name if it were a girl.

Blake smiles softly and says, "Connor."

The nurse lets Connor sleep on my chest for a little while longer before pulling him off and carrying him over to the scale where she also wipes him off. I watch with rapt attention as she moves him around, wanting to make sure everything goes okay, and my heart presses against my chest.

There's no room for anything else. This, right here, is what I needed to feel complete. I've got the family I've always dreamed of and that brings a smile to my face, which only gets brighter when Arabella finally makes it to visit a couple hours later.

She's going to be a natural as a big sister. And Blake? Well, let's just say Connor already has him wrapped around his very tiny finger.

The End.

Did you like this book? Then you'll LOVE "Snowed In with my Ex's Dad".

I needed a distraction from my recent divorce, but waking up naked next to my ex-lover's father was not my plan.

Divorcing Connor took me far too long. I need him to change, but his anger from his own parent's divorce caused a divide we could never recover from.

Declan only wanted to mend his relationship with his son. While Connor continued to refuse all contact with his father.

It was pure coincidence that Declan and I both resorted to a few days of solitude in the mountains. Getting double-booked in the same cabin meant trouble.

The ecstasy I reached that single night with Declan far exceeded any moment with Connor.

Lying naked with my ex's father should feel sinful and wrong. Yet my entire being yearns for Declan's pleasurable touch to envelope every inch of my body once more.

I know we can't allow this to happen again or Connor will never forgive his father. I just don't know how I'm going to explain what's coming in 9 months.

Start reading "Snowed In with my Ex's Dad" NOW!

https://www.amazon.com/dp/B0CCSG8LGM

Sneak Peek - Chapter One
Start reading "Snowed In with my Ex's Dad" NOW!

Chapter One

Declan

The crunching snow beneath my feet makes me grunt in frustration at the impending snowstorm headed this way. You'd think after living my life in this godforsaken state that I'd grow accustomed to the snowstorms that come with it, but that's definitely not the case.

The front office for check in at the cabins is only a few feet away, but before I get on the steps, my foot finds a sheet of black ice and I feel my legs start to give way under me. Luckily, I grab hold of the banister just in time to catch the fall.

"Stupid snow," I mutter to myself, but a woman chuckles low behind me. Since I don't want to be rude, I choose to ignore her, not even bothering to glance back at her, and continue my trek into the warmth of the office.

The receptionist smiles brightly at me, gazing approvingly at my body before fluttering her eyelashes. She's definitely younger than me, and the way her lips tip up in a smirk that she thinks is sexy only freaks me out.

I thrust my card into her freshly manicured fingers. "Baker," I snap, fed up with the way this day is already going for me and wanting to get into my cabin to relax. A hot shower sounds more than fantastic right now, but this woman seems to want to take her time and it only infuriates me more.

She's purposely going slower, trying to catch my attention by bending over the counter and pushing her breasts right in my line of vision. I catch the swell of them, but her assets are the least of my worries right now. Instead of giving her the satisfaction of looking at what she's offering me, I choose to glare at her in hopes that she will speed up her process.

"I'd like to get into my cabin any day now," I grumble at her.

She flinches at my tone, but it hits her the way I intended and she starts typing furiously on the computer. Her hand swings back, grabbing hold of a key just for me, and slaps it down on the flat countertop. When I nod my thanks to her, the only thing she does is sneer at me before throwing her attention to the phone lighting up in front of her.

Oh well, I can't quite seem to care if she expected more from me. I might be a single father, but I'm definitely not on the market. I learned the hard way that women will leave you when you least expect it, and the way that affects your life. My son's mother was everything I wanted in a woman, until she wasn't. It wasn't my fault our relationship ended, but our son doesn't miss the chance to blame it on me any chance he gets.

I'm not even sure what he thinks happened between me and his mom, just that I'm the brunt of all his anger and it's damaged our relationship more than I'd like. When I reach the red wooden door of my cabin, I walk inside and inhale the cedar scent wafting throughout the place. These log cabins are my favorite getaway, even if the only thing I can see outside my window right now is snow-covered ground.

Nothing will ever beat the view of the snow-capped mountains from this point, which is exactly why I request this cabin every single time I come here. Sure, all the other ones have a view of the mountain just as I do, but most of their views involve trees blocking it a bit. Mine though? There are a few trees that I can see in front of the mountain, but for the most part, I have an optimal view of the peaks ahead

I reach into my pocket, connect my phone to the built-in Wi-Fi since I don't get service in this area, and open Facebook. When I check Messenger, it shows Connor is online and I try to give him a call, hoping that he will answer, but he lets it ring through.

Shower. That's what I need.

There's a fresh stack of towels piled high on the rack in the bathroom, along with a pile of washcloths, and I appreciate that they've accounted for the snowstorm coming in. I called ahead, letting them know that I ordered delivery from the local grocery store so that I'd have food stocked just in case and I glance through everything. At least they had the manners to put everything away for me, I can respect that at least.

I check my phone one more time, releasing a defeated sigh when I don't have any calls back from Connor. If he'd give me the time of day, I'd be able to talk to him about my situation with his mom. If there's anyone to blame for our split, it's *her*, considering she was in bed with one of her clients. He refuses to listen to me, but that won't stop me from trying.

The bathroom door is open all the way, the light shining from it, and it's calling my name. The hot water will wash away all my worries. I slip my shoes off right next to the door, then pull my socks off and throw them into the foldable cloth hamper I always bring with me. The rest of my clothes take time to remove, and once I'm standing gloriously naked in the middle of the cabin, the suffocation I'm feeling eases slightly.

The wooden floor is cool beneath my feet when I walk into the bathroom, prompting me to power the small space heater up that's standing in one corner of the room. I groan at the heat pushing onto my feet, then pad across the floor to turn the shower's water on, cranking the heat all the way up. With both the steam and the heat from the space heater, the room is starting to feel cozy already.

I grab one of the towels, placing it about a foot away from the heater, letting it warm up for when I go to wrap it around me, and step into the shower's hot spray.

It scolds me, like it's burning through each layer of my skin, and I clench my teeth at the pain. Once the sting wears away, I lean my head back and thread my fingers through my dark strands. Most men my age choose to keep their hair short and clean-shaven. I'm not like most men my age though and prefer a neatly shaved beard and my hair long.

I'm a proud believer in keeping my body in shape, which is why you'll see me at the gym daily, and eating as healthy as possible. I'll have a cheat day every now and then, but not as often as most people. The green smoothie I drink every morning causes most people to look at me in disgust and it brings me much-needed amusement every time.

The water is starting to get cooler and I shut the shower head off, then step out of the shower. My towel on the floor is warmed up, feeling great when I wrap it around my hips, and I walk over to the bathroom mirror. I wipe through the fog, staring at the redness of my skin from the shower before casting my gaze over to the toothbrush sitting on the back of the sink.

I grab it, slathering a layer of toothpaste onto the bristles, and watch my reflection as I brush back and forth. As the redness starts to fade away, I catch sight of my sun-kissed skin that's slowly beginning to fade.

Unfortunately, I haven't had much spare time out in the sun and it shows. I'm not some uptight older man, but I love my body looking a certain way, a way that makes me feel better about myself, and I don't believe there's anything wrong with that.

My stomach rumbles, clueing me into the amount of food I haven't eaten today, and I push away from the sink. I figure since I'm in this place all alone, walking around in a towel for a while wouldn't be so bad. Instead of getting dressed, I head straight for the kitchen to find something to make to eat. I'm tired, so I'll probably go with something simple like spaghetti or chicken Alfredo.

The thought of chicken Alfredo appeals to me, so I gather everything I need for that and get the water heated on the stove. Once the noodles start cooking, I fry up the chicken in a skillet before cutting them into bite-sized pieces and throwing them back in with two jars of Alfredo sauce. Yes, I'm one of those people who use canned ingredients because I'm too lazy to make my own homemade stuff. I won't feel bad about that.

This will probably count as a cheat meal. Granted, I usually count the entire week that I'm here as a cheat day since there are usually storms that come in to keep me from getting my healthier stuff. I stalked up on some stuff to have a salad or two every day, at least, so that's a plus side to everything. When the sauce starts to boil, I drain the noodles and fix myself a plate.

Just as I'm lifting the fork to my mouth, ready to take a steaming hot bite of my food, the door to the cabin bursts open and a woman stands at the entrance. Her head is turned back, focused solely on pulling her suitcase through the door, and she doesn't notice me sitting there yet.

Who the hell is this?

That's answered for me when she finally turns around, eyes widening at my half-naked figure sitting at the edge of the brown leather sofa. There's a black and red plaid blanket hanging on the back of the couch, calling out for me to sling it over my lap, but I can't seem to pay attention to it. Not when my son's ex-wife is standing in front of me, looking absolutely sinful in her tight jeans and thick light pink sweater.

"What are you doing here?" she asks, her lips pursing in annoyance, and that only has me thinking about what her lips might taste like.

I stand from my spot on the couch, the towel still tightly tied around my waist, and lean against the kitchen counter while holding my plate of food. "Uh, eating?"

My smirk doesn't bring one out of her and she blows a loud breath out, turning around to leave the cabin.

"Wait," I say, looking down at all the extra food I know I'm going to have left and not wanting to waste it. "At least eat something while you're already here."

She stares at me with a blank expression on her face, her eyes tracing the lines of my muscles, and that only causes my dick to stir. Unfortunately for me, these towels aren't the biggest or thickest, so the moment I stand at attention she catches the movement.

This is a terrible idea, but I can't take back the offer now. She looks like she's having a hard day and I feel like she might enjoy some company right now. When she sinks her teeth into her bottom lip, I almost say fuck it and take long strides over to her to slam my lips to hers, but I keep my feet glued to my spot.

"Uh, yeah," she agrees somewhat tentatively, "food sounds nice right now."

She leans her suitcase against the wall close to the door, then slips her boots off before walking across the room and grabbing the plate I'm holding out for her. "Thank you," she whispers, staring right at my lips as she does, before darting her gaze away.

The knuckles clutching my plate are turning white from my grip on it and I turn around so that I'm not watching her as she eats. The moment she lets out a small moan after taking a bite, I can't help but rush to close the distance between us.

This is such a bad idea, but I can't seem to care right now.

Start reading "Snowed In with my Ex's Dad" NOW!

https://www.amazon.com/dp/B0CCSG8LGM

Do you like FREEBIE Romance books?
Sign up for my newsletter and get "Riding High On Love" for free!

Saving the single Dad cowboy sounds like a fairytale opposites-attract romance. Too bad I'm here to take his ranch.

I needed a fresh start. My career is in turmoil and won't last if I don't close this deal.

This shouldn't be difficult. Graham's ranch is floundering and he has a lot to manage in his personal life. But it's harder than I thought.

My affection for Graham grows deeper every day. He is so tender with his daughter while caring for his dying father. This wasn't supposed to happen to me.

The night Graham saves me from an over-aggressive playboy at the local bar seals my desire for him. Shivers of pleasure run down my spine as I relive the intense passion of the greatest night of my life.

Now I stand at the crossroads of my career and my heart.

<u>Sign Up Now!</u>
https://dl.bookfunnel.com/fazewgs4k8

Want to see the rest of my books?
<u>Go HERE!</u>
https://www.amazon.com/stores/Nic-Spade/author/B0C9WJY97L

Made in the USA
Middletown, DE
03 November 2023